RADIO SILENCE

Alyssa Cole

Also by Alyssa Cole

Signal Boost (Off the Grid book 2)

Mixed Signals (Off the Grid book 2)

Eagle's Heart

Agnes Moor's Wild Knight

Be Not Afraid

Let It Shine

RADIO SILENCE
Copyright © 2015 by Alyssa Cole
All rights reserved,
including the right of reproduction
in whole or in part in any form.

Edited by Rhonda Stapleton

ISBN-13: 978-1539664666
ISBN-10: 153966466X

For Nicolas, awesome husband and number-one draft pick for my post-apocalyptic survival squad.

Most people are perfectly afraid of silence.

-e.e. cummings

1

So much blood.

The Louisville Slugger stung my palms as it was ripped from my hands. I felt my backpack being pulled off and my arms yanked roughly behind me, but my gaze was fixed on John, who lay unmoving on the frozen ground.

The snow around his head was a slushy pink corona, growing at an incomprehensibly fast rate as blood seeped from his wound. His thick black hair had fallen over his face; in the fading afternoon light I could see it was slicked down, his blood serving as a ghastly pomade.

Even though it was well below freezing and I had been chilled to the bone for days, I broke out in a sweat. After the sweat came the nausea and the dizziness. The snow glared blindingly white, and the tall conifers that had so recently provided shelter now seemed to be closing in on me.

When the electricity had gone, followed by the heat, plumbing and water, I'd been worried. When our food supply had begun to dwindle and we'd decided to trek a hundred miles to John's parents' cabin near the Canadian border, I'd been scared shitless. What I felt as I watched my best friend bleed out before my eyes was terror, pure and undiluted.

I shook my head and gulped in mouthfuls of cold air. I couldn't faint, despite the ever-increasing pool of blood around John's head and the way his arms and legs were unnaturally splayed.

It was unbearable seeing him so still. I was used to his constant motion; John was like a windup toy whose gears never stopped moving. It annoyed some people, but I'd loved it about him from the instant he showed up at my front door, sizing me up as if I was trying to move into *his* apartment instead of the other way around. He had smiled and extended his hand to me, his grip much stronger than his birdlike frame let on.

"I'm a complete control freak, so I'll probably want to handle the utility bills and may pick out your shoes for you, if the mood strikes," he'd warned me. "But those things aren't going to happen because I'm gaysian."

"Well, I sometimes get irrationally angry and I love fried chicken," I'd replied. "But that's not because I'm black, it's because people are annoying and chicken is delicious."

"Oh, Arden, we're going to be the best roommates ever," he'd gushed, flashing me his Cheshire cat grin. "Our memoirs will be called *Collard Greens and Kimchi: A Love Story.* I can see it now."

"Looks like you and your friend made a wrong turn." The man who'd taken John down spoke, pulling my mind back to the horror show we had unwittingly become a part of.

The blond hair that stuck out from under his blue woolen hat was stringy and unwashed, and although he was a big man, his coat looked about a size too large for him. He unstrapped a foldable slingshot from his arm, shoving it into one of his deep pockets. It seemed impossible that the flimsy neon contraption had hurt John, but the large rock that had rebounded off his skull had been sturdy enough.

Blue Hat nudged John with his boot-clad foot, rolling him onto his side. John's lips were blue, and snow clung to the scraggly tufts of hair that were the closest he would ever get to a beard. Minutes ago his cheeks had been ruddy from exertion; now he looked like a frozen corpse.

Panic welled up in me and I struggled against the other man, the one who held both of my arms twisted behind my back. He grunted and kicked at the back of my knees, activating a reflex that made my legs buckle. My knees hovered just above the ground, arching my back at a painful angle, but my captor refused to loosen his grip. I struggled, despite the pain in my shoulders.

I finally spoke.

"A person's sense of direction tends to get fucked up when they're freezing and starving." A long beat had passed between Blue Hat's observation and my response. My mind was operating on a delay, looping back to the need to get to John at the expense of my other functions.

Blue Hat graced me with a sharp look. Now I had his attention, but not for the reason I wanted. The way his eyes skimmed over my body revealed that my voice had given away what my bulky down jacket and large hood had been hiding.

"We're well acquainted with freezing and starving both, sweetie," he said. His words were bleak, but there was something liquid and insinuating in his voice that hadn't been there before. "We've gone without a lot of things since the lights went out."

"We don't have anything valuable," I said, slowly snapping out of my stupor. "We've got nothing but peanut shells. Why don't you just let us go and we can all pretend we never crossed paths?"

John's head lolled from side to side as Blue Hat grabbed his backpack and shook it free. John performed a sickening version of a marionette dance before crumpling back to the ground. Anger flared bright and fast in my chest, fueled by the knowledge that there was nothing I could do but look on impotently. I held my body still, although I longed to fight my way free. Struggling only made the man behind me tighten his hold.

"We're just two people trying to survive, like you," I continued, hoping to appeal to their sense of humanity, but Blue Hat ignored me and busied himself with unzipping John's backpack and rifling through it.

John and I had known things were bad, had purposely avoided other people during our trek, but it still seemed unreal that these men were so comfortable with assaulting us. The blackout had only happened three weeks ago. Was that how little time it took for a man to lose his moral compass?

"Just like us, except you have provisions and we don't." The man pulled a peanut out of John's bag, cracked the shell and tossed the nut into his mouth. He looked up at me and grinned. "Well, that's not true. Now we do."

He held my gaze, and I felt my stomach flip. There was something in the way his grin kept going, widening into the unnatural toothiness of a shark that's scented blood, that alerted me to the change in his thought pattern. An instinctive female warning bell sounded in my head when he graced me with that smile.

"I'll bite your dick off if you even think about it," I snarled. My voice sounded strong, but my stomach twisted with fear when the man behind me pulled me closer to his body.

Blue Hat chuckled; he seemed to get a rise out of the challenge, so I tried another approach. He was likely the kind of guy who would be more amenable to a woman who made him feel big. I hated to do it, but I dropped the brashness from my voice, pleading with him. I didn't have to fake the tremor in my voice. "John's family lives around here. They could be your neighbors or friends."

I regretted the words even as they slipped out of my mouth. John's parents owned a grocery store in the area, and given Blue Hat's fixation on getting supplies, it was probably best he didn't associate us with the Seongs.

"You hurt him really badly." My voice cracked, and I had to swallow hard around the lump in my throat before I could continue. "Please just take our stuff and let us go so I can help him."

"I don't think so, sweetheart. The way I see it, you and your little friend count as provisions too."

"What?" I couldn't help the strangled, ugly noise that came out of my throat. He couldn't mean what I thought he meant, could he?

John, please get up! You would know what to do right now. He had a knack for sizing up a situation and acting accordingly, whereas I endlessly annoyed him with my impulsive, occasionally irrational decision-making.

But John remained still and, for the first time, I allowed the possibility that he might be dead to take root. My best friend could be dead or dying, these men had no intention of letting us go and we were in this position because of me. Because of the impatience John always chided me about. I glanced at him and wished I'd listened to him for once, but I figured even he would have agreed that logic couldn't help us at this point.

Before I had time to dissuade myself, I rocked onto the balls of my feet and sprang back, using every ounce of force I could muster. White-hot pain seared through my back when my arms tore from the man's grip, but I achieved my goal of knocking my unseen captor off his feet. I scrambled to my feet and turned quickly, landing a solid kick to the man's face as he tried to get up, and then another, and another, ignoring the sickening crunch of his nose giving way beneath my boot. I channeled the sick anger and fear that roiled my gut into those kicks, and they had the intended result. The tread of my Doc Martens left a visible imprint on the man's bloody face, and he'd stopped trying to get up. I was turning to deal with Blue Hat when I was tackled from behind.

"You little bitch," Blue Hat snarled into my ear while I struggled to stay on my feet and free myself from the bear hug that locked my arms at my side. My bulky jacket didn't help matters, and I wished I'd kept my pepper spray handy like I had for the first part of the hike, before we got to this more sparsely populated area where I became complacent.

I tried to remain upright, panic surging through me at the thought of being on the ground under this man. He overpowered me using brute force, though, pulling my legs out from under me and falling forward. Gravity did the rest. My face smashed into the icy shards of snow as Blue Hat's weight crashed down on top of me. The wind was knocked out of me, and for a long, terrifying moment I couldn't breathe as my lungs constricted with pain.

But then I was able to manage one breath, and a larger one after. The shock of the impact faded, and I began thrashing like a fish on a hook that has no intention of being anyone's dinner. I couldn't break his iron hold or escape from the sour smell of his hair and the rancid odor of his breath. He panted from the exertion, and each foul cloud of condensation was a reminder of what he would do to me if I gave up. I struggled, powered by a fresh surge of panic, but it was fruitless; in this position, there was nothing I could do to escape his grasp.

"Get off me!" I managed to raise my head and bellow, hoping it would throw him off guard. My voice rang out into the silence of the snow-covered trees and then disappeared, with no effect on him. Instead, he flipped me over onto my back and sat on my chest, crushing my already aching lungs. His knees pinned down my arms and when I tried to scream again, in spite of his weight on top of me, he punched me so hard that I saw little pinpricks of light dancing before my eyes. A double whammy of pain flared in my skull, radiating from my jaw and overlapping with the pain surging from where the back of my head slammed into the ground. Tears formed in my eyes and were already ice-cold before they slid down my cheeks.

"The little ones are always feisty," he said with a chuckle, and then hauled off and punched me once more, for emphasis. "Now quit squirming. Unless you want me to do that again."

He loomed over me, backlit against the darkening winter sky. His mouth was twisted into a sneer but his eyes were bright with what seemed like enjoyment. I thought of experiments I'd read about, where people were told that if they pushed a button they would cause someone in another room extreme pain. So many seemingly normal people had pushed that button, repeatedly and with delight.

I'm sorry, John. Maybe it's better if you don't wake up.

Blue Hat's eyes moved from my face to the stand of trees John and I had emerged from. I heard movement, the muffled crunch of heavy boots on snow. A deep, rich voice, tinged with horror, sounded from somewhere out of my line of sight.

"John?"

And just as Blue Hat began shifting off me to charge forward, just as I felt air flooding my lungs and a strange floating sensation of freedom in my arms and chest, I heard the cock of a gun and the blast of a shot. Blue Hat flew off me and landed in the snow at my feet. He flailed a bit, trying to bring his hands to the hole in his chest, but then his arms dropped to his sides and he was still. The other man struggled to sit up and made an ungainly move for his pocket, but he fumbled and another blast laid him out too.

My ears rang in the silence that followed the gunshots and I swallowed against the panicked whimpers that tried to escape my mouth. I scrambled away from the body of my would-be kidnapper. His legs tangled with mine as I fled, as if he was trying to keep me down with him.

The man who'd saved us from unknown horrors was lanky and broad-shouldered, dressed all in black, and his face was covered by a ski mask that made him look a hundred times more frightening than Blue Hat and his friend. But then he dropped his rifle and pulled off the balaclava, and there was a face so similar to John's that I gasped. He was older than John's twenty-four years, and his features were more rugged, but he had those same gently sloping eyes, the same furrow that formed between the brows when John was upset. His black hair was shorter than John's, but long enough to hang shaggy over his ears, wavy instead of pin-straight.

He ran over to John's prone form and dropped to his knees. "Shit, this can't be happening. I can't lose you too. Fuck," the man who had to be John's brother muttered.

What was his name? Gabriel? My mind was reeling, but then it came back to me. Yes, there was Gabriel, who was two years out from med school and always too busy to visit. And there was a sister, Maggie, who was a junior in high school.

That meant we were close to our destination. John had told me we were, but I hadn't believed him after asking "Are we there yet?" for the hundredth time. I'd led us straight into trouble instead.

Gabriel grabbed John's wrist and checked his pulse, and then trotted over to me. "Are you okay? Did they hurt you too?" His eyes were wide, pupils darting back and forth as if he was running some kind of medical scan in his mind.

Up close, he wasn't as similar to John as I'd thought. His build was athletic and not simply thin. His clean-shaven face was all angles: high cheekbones and a square jaw. He possessed a kind of lean hungriness that stood in stark contrast to John's boyish good looks.

The biggest difference was their eyes. John's were

nearly the same dark brown as mine, but Gabriel's were so light they seemed golden, his irises rimmed with black.

"I got hit a couple of times, but I'm fine, thanks to you," I said, although pain radiated throughout my body when he helped me to my feet. He swept his hands over my cheeks and then prodded my jaw. The pressure of his cold fingertips felt good against my battered face. I knew it was completely inappropriate, given the circumstances, but still—I couldn't help that his touch sent little frissons of pleasure through me. Maybe lack of human contact besides John for weeks had done something to me. Without thinking, I pressed my face into his hand, seeking the innate comfort of his touch.

His eyes lingered on mine for a long moment, and something flashed in the honey-colored depths, but the concerned grimace never left his lips. "You seem to be okay. Can you grab one of those guys' scarves or something and bring it over here?" he asked, abruptly breaking contact with me to return to John. It was more of a command than a request; he seemed comfortable giving orders, and I was happy to follow them at this point.

I ran over to Blue Hat and tried not to look into his glassy eyes as I picked up his scarf, which had come off during our struggle, with trembling hands. The pool of blood forming around him was much larger than the one around John, and only then did I notice that the front of my coat was a Pollock in miniature, red droplets splattered over the taupe material. I realized that Gabriel had been wiping blood off my face when he first touched me, blood that wasn't my own. My head swam and my legs nearly gave out, but I stumbled away from the body and handed off the scarf. I sank to my knees beside Gabriel while he used snow to clean the blood away from John's head and pinpoint the wound's location.

"Can I help?" I asked. He pulled out a pocketknife and sliced off a section of the scarf.

"Apply pressure here." He placed the balled fabric over the wound to stanch the bleeding, and I laid my trembling hands over it, afraid that I would hurt John. Gabriel covered my hands with one of his own and pressed down hard, letting me feel the right amount of pressure, before turning his full attention to his brother.

"John, can you hear me?" he asked. He got no response. I felt another flash of dizziness at the thought that John might not be all right, but I made sure to hold the fabric firmly. It was the only thing I could do to help him now.

John, please be okay.

"I can't believe I found you. How did you guys get here?" he asked. He pulled at John's eyelids and examined each pupil, and then wrapped John's head with the remainder of the scarf to secure the makeshift bandage in place.

"We walked from Rochester," I said through chattering teeth. Now that a few moments had passed, fatigue crept up on me; a more frightening sensation loomed when I thought of the bodies that littered the ground around us, so I tried to ignore them. "The roads are clear up here since it's the middle of nowhere, but they're packed with abandoned cars near the more populated areas. Without traffic lights, the accidents piled up fast and thick."

"I meant what are you guys doing, here, in this part of the woods?" he asked. "If you were walking from Rochester, you should have been coming from the other direction."

"Shouldn't we get moving?" I didn't want to answer his question, and something in my voice gave me away.

Gabriel pulled his gloves back on, regarding me with a new look in his eyes, one that I didn't like at all. "John knows how to read maps. He can navigate using the stars and he knows these woods. How did you end up off course?" His complete calm was somehow more terrifying than if he had grabbed my collar and demanded answers.

"I—I—" I was shaking too hard to answer the question, too overcome with guilt to speak the words. I could have lied, but I'd disappointed my mother enough for one lifetime. I finally spit it out. "It was my fault," I said, meeting his gaze. "John kept telling me we were almost there, for hours. I snapped. I got angry and said I wanted to lead for a while. I took the map and the compass from him and led us the wrong way."

I sat there trembling with my chin pointed up in the air while he stared at me as if I was the biggest idiot he'd ever laid eyes on. Normally, I couldn't care less if someone liked me or thought I was stupid, especially someone I'd known for all of five minutes, but having Gabriel look at me like that hurt. I knew I'd been wrong, but I really wished he didn't have to know it too.

"So you're telling me that instead of listening to my

brother, who was an Eagle Scout, who played orienteering games with my father in these very woods and who was leading you to *his* family's house, you decided you would take over and lead the way. Why did this seem like a good idea to you?"

All of the adrenaline that had fueled my failed escape attempt drained out of me, and when I spoke my voice was thin and ragged. "I didn't want this to happen. I was just so tired of walking and walking and not knowing what was going on."

With a sound of disgust, he stood and moved away from me. He picked up John's pack and swung it onto his back, and then handed me mine, which was heavier than I remembered. "I don't have time for this. Can you carry the gun without accidentally shooting me or my brother?" he asked as he put the safety on the rifle and handed it to me. He added, as though it was an afterthought, "Or yourself?"

I shrugged on my pack before scrambling to my feet and grabbing the gun. It, too, was heavier than it appeared. "Might not want to be a jerk to the girl with the firearm," I muttered.

He scooped up John and started heading back into the woods. When he paused and turned back, I expected him to berate me some more. Instead, his gaze passed me to observe the bodies of the two men he'd shot. He stared for a long time, his expression softening as the anger left him and was replaced with a heartrending sadness.

I didn't need to look back; the image would be

etched into my mind forever. I gripped the gun, realizing that Gabriel had done what I couldn't and that he'd be the one to have to live with it. The thought was an additional burden, sapping strength from me with its immensity.

"Come on," he said, and then took off into the trees at a brisk pace.

I couldn't stop shivering—my face throbbed, my body ached and Gabriel blamed me for John's condition—but at least after days spent camping in the woods and hiding from every human we saw, we were about to reach our destination. I hoped John would be well enough to enjoy our success.

"Is he going to be all right?" I asked in a voice that sounded tiny and distant. Now that we had started walking, my head felt like a tethered balloon and I just wanted to sit down. I also wanted a hug, and my mom, in no particular order. What I got was a hard look from Gabriel.

He turned away from me and continued at his fast clip, despite being weighed down by his brother. His movements were lithe, reminding me of the way a big cat moves through the jungle. I stumbled behind him, clumsily knocking into every tree in my path as I tried to keep up. Perhaps letting me hold the gun hadn't been the best decision.

"I hope so," Gabriel said. "It's not good that he's still unconscious, but the wound doesn't seem life-threatening."

There was something about the timbre of his voice that projected an appealing sense of surety. If he'd told me everything was going to be fine, that our ordeal was over and I didn't have to worry, I would've believed him without hesitation. But his next words were delivered with a cold directness that denied any offer of comfort.

"But you never know with head injuries. If he isn't okay, I'm placing the blame on you."

There was at least one thing we could agree on, then.

I followed him in silence. Each step seemed to sap more energy from me than normal, but I pushed myself forward with the thought that the cabin had to be close. Besides, despite his initial concern over me, I didn't think Gabriel would be very sympathetic if I told him I wasn't feeling so hot.

I glanced up and hoped we would arrive soon. The auroras were already starting to show against the darkening skies. Before the blackout, I'd always wanted to see the beautiful phenomenon, planning imaginary trips to Alaska and Iceland I couldn't afford. Now my wish had come true like something from a djinni tale. The aurora had blazed every night since the blackout, its vivid undulations a reminder that we were in truly deep shit.

After what seemed like miles of walking through the heavily wooded area, the trees started to thin and we stepped out into a small clearing. In the middle of the clearing was the love child of a cabin and a McMansion. The large house was shingled in dark wood and accented with green trim over the windows and doors. A thin line of smoke spiraled from the chimney, signaling that warmth and comfort awaited us. I knew we'd arrived at our destination, but it still seemed like a mirage amid the pines. Then I noticed the windows all along the first floor had been boarded up and I realized the house was all too real.

The door opened, and a girl stepped onto the porch. She was tall and straight-backed like Gabriel, her round face nearly hidden by long, side-swept bangs. Her hand flew to her mouth at the sight of John in Gabriel's arms, and she ran from the porch toward us, her hair floating behind her like a dark curtain.

She was the last thing I saw before dropping the gun and face-planting into the snow.

2

"Arden."

I heard my name and wanted to respond, but I was pulling myself out of the deepest sublevel of sleep, the kind you woke up from feeling drugged and disoriented, stumbling if you stood too quickly.

"Wake up, Arden."

Why was John bothering me? He was well aware I didn't like to be disturbed before my alarm went off. Wait. Why hadn't my alarm sounded?

A hazy memory floated to the surface of my semi-lucid mind: John and I lounging in the living room of our apartment. We clutched mugs of eggnog and watched the saber rattling on the nightly news, where they recapped the now-routine Russian threats against the West. The light-bulbs flared out with a *pop!* and the image on our sleek TV flattened to a thin white line, leaving us in total darkness. The glow of two signalless cell phones illuminated our confused faces. We cranked the hand-operated emergency radio John had insisted we buy, but it only produced an eerie white noise more chilling than a panicked announcement of impending attack would've been.

"Arden."

Reality clicked into place just as something icy and wet landed on my face. I bolted upright, spluttering and trying to paw the cold slush out of my nose and mouth.

It was only when I dragged a blanket across my face that I realized I was in a bed and not on the cold, hard ground. It wasn't my own, but a twin-size bed with sky-blue sheets and a thick comforter to match. The sheets smelled like detergent, which was akin to a miracle after going days without fresh clothing.

Across the room, under a giant poster of Wayne Gretzky that could only be described as vintage, John sat propped up in a twin bed that mirrored mine. His head was wrapped with a large white bandage, but other than that, he looked clean and in good health. In fact, he was humming happily as he reached into a bucket next to his bed and began packing another snowball.

"Oh. Hey there, Arden. Nice to see you're finally up after a bazillion hours of sleep," he said. "I was starting to think *you* were the one with the head injury."

He dropped the snowball into a sandwich bag that rested in his lap, sealed the bag and held the compress against his head, smiling at me as if he hadn't been unconscious and bleeding the last time I'd seen him.

A burst of elation cartwheeled through me. John, who may have been the only person left I could call family, was alive and, by all appearances, well. I burst into tears of relief, jumping out of my bed and closing the short distance between us. I ignored the soreness in my shins and how one side of my face throbbed as I bounced across the room. I put the brakes on before tackling him and instead pivoted and sat on the side of the bed, grabbing his free hand and squeezing it.

"Wow. The only time I've ever seen you cry is at the end of *Marley & Me*," he said. "You really do love me, huh?"

"I'm sorry—" I bit my quivering lower lip and swallowed against the sudden obstruction in my throat, unable to continue.

"Don't be silly," he said. "When you threw your hissy fit, you couldn't have known you'd lead us straight toward some crazed mountain men."

The pain in my chest receded a little, just a little, knowing that John didn't blame me even if I blamed myself. Then a deep, knife-sharp voice interrupted our moment, cutting through my happiness and shredding my temporary relief.

"You're lucky those men were armed with a slingshot instead of a gun." Gabriel's words sounded against the guilt that sat heavy in my heart, and the emotion resonated through me.

I turned to see him leaning against the door frame. His arms were folded casually across his chest, as if we were having a pleasant chat, but the glare he shot me undercut his demeanor. I wondered if he realized he was looking at me as though I'd hit John in the head myself, or if he disliked me so much that he couldn't rein in his facial expressions. I remembered his soft touch in the forest and wondered who that person had been, because this guy seemed hell-bent on making me suffer.

"Yes, quite lucky. But I'm going to be okay," John said. He punctuated his words with jazz hands. His tone treaded a thin line between saccharine and shut-the-fuck-up, an ability I'd always admired. "Considering that no one even knows what the hell is going on in the world, we may have bigger problems to worry about. So we should really all try to get along."

Gabriel shifted position, squaring his shoulders and shoving his hands into his jeans pockets. Without my permission, my gaze skittered over the muscled torso delineated under his tight-fitting black henley shirt. I was torn between wishing he wasn't right and wishing he wasn't so freaking smug about it. Since three wishes were standard, I also wished he wasn't so damned attractive while glowering at me.

Et tu, libido?

"As long as certain people know their place and don't make stupid decisions that could get others hurt, then we should all get along just fine," he said, still looking at me. His rosy lips were pressed into a thin line, but the hint of a smirk played at the corners.

I wiped my tears away and returned his glare. Sure, I felt like a shitty friend for leading John astray, but letting Gabriel dictate my behavior wasn't part of my groveling-for-forgiveness plan. "If we're going to discuss people knowing their places, let's get one thing straight," I said, trying to keep my voice low and measured. Even if he was being a jerk, he *had* saved my life, so I wouldn't give him full-blast attitude. "I appreciate the hospitality, but I have enough stress to deal with, like the apocalypse or *Red Dawn: Part Two* or whatever the hell is going on. I don't need to add 'control freak asshole' to the list."

Gabriel narrowed his hooded eyes at me, and then shifted his gaze to John, who had settled back against his pillows and was observing the exchange as if watching a tennis match.

"I'm sure you can see why I'm smitten by her," John said to Gabriel, and nudged me with his knee. "He's just a little uptight. He'll grow on you, I promise."

"Like mold?" I asked with a sniff.

John chuckled. "No," he said and paused to think. "More like that mouse that used to invade our kitchen every night. Remember how much you hated that thing?"

"He ate my peanut butter cups," I said. "The penalty for that is death."

"Yes, but then one day you saw those cute little eyes peering up at you as he scampered across the stove top. Next thing I knew, you wanted to catch the germ-ridden thing and keep it for a pet."

"It was a wild gerbil, okay, not some diseased city mouse," I said petulantly, remembering the silly box-and-string trap John had rigged up for me, and how we'd been so busy laughing we hadn't noticed the mouse run by and snag the peanut butter-laden cracker we'd used for bait.

"Hopefully, we'll have some idea of what's going on soon," Gabriel said. "If we don't, I'm pretty sure being stuck in a house with the affirmative-action version of *Will & Grace* will drive me crazy."

The joke caught me by surprise. I snorted, not wanting to give him the satisfaction of my laughter.

He walked past me and squatted beside the bed. After unwrapping the bandage around John's head, he began an examination of the wound. There was something so tender in the way he cradled his brother's head that I had to turn away. I didn't want to consider the kinder, gentler facets of himself that Gabriel bestowed upon John while he was treating me like something he'd stepped in and tracked home.

"I'm glad you made it to the house," he said as he re-wrapped the bandage. "We hoped you would come. It was torture not knowing how you were faring, and then finding you like that..."

"I know. I'm just happy you guys are okay and we're all together now," John said, sighing deeply.

I pushed down my envy. I had no idea whether my parents were okay, and the probability of being together with them was nil.

Gabriel closed his eyes and tilted his head from one side to the other, something I did when tension locked the muscles in my neck. When he wasn't busy tending to John or making it clear that he didn't like me, it was plain to see that he was bone-tired.

"I didn't know what we'd find if we made it here." John grabbed a section of blanket and absentmindedly twisted it as he talked. "The worst part about all this isn't just losing electricity and access to clean water, or wondering if your neighbor has gone crazy and is willing to kill you for some ramen noodles. It's going through all of that and not even knowing why."

He stared down at the floor, and I knew he was thinking of the things that had driven us from our apartment in Rochester, besides the lack of food. Thousands of people living together without working plumbing, access to water and well-stocked food sources may have worked in the past, but modern people were accustomed to having nearly every whim accessible, every question answerable by their smartphone. When that was snatched away from us, society at large had begun to unspool pretty quickly.

"I know," I said. "If you told me that the reason I hadn't showered in weeks was because aliens had landed or World War III was in full effect, I could at least put my B.O. in context."

"Yeah, the bathroom is at the end of the hall, to the right. I asked Maggie to set some stuff up in there for you," Gabriel said. I was suddenly aware of how close he was to said B.O., and my indignation rose at there being yet another thing he could judge me for. "The house has a generator, so we have heat and electricity, but we're trying to limit the usage since we don't know how long this will last. If you get cold, put on another sweater—no touching the thermostat. And take a bath instead of a shower. I'm talking a birdbath, not a Calgon soak. It doesn't take too much water to get clean."

Even with Gabriel's restrictions laid down, I wanted that bath more than anything in the world. When the electricity had first gone, so had the hot water—soon after, the taps had run dry. Aside from scrubbing myself with baby wipes, I hadn't been able to really wash myself in weeks.

"Okay, boss man," I muttered, and then turned to John. "It'll be nice to meet your sister. Hopefully, her disposition is closer to yours."

A memory surfaced then, a girl with a fall of black hair running from the house and into the cold before everything went dark.

"She was in here creepily staring at you when I woke

up earlier," John said. "Apparently, you're her new hero since Gabriel told her you took on the two guys who attacked us. It's kind of sweet. Don't worry, I warned her not to touch your hair unless she wanted to pull back a stump."

I put my hand up to the frizzy, matted mess on my head. Before this ordeal had begun, it had been a mass of soft, tight curls that rested on my shoulders. People's hands had always been drawn to it, whether I wanted their caresses or not.

"Anyone who wants to touch this rat's nest right now would have to be really crazy. It'll be nice to meet her though. And your parents."

Gabriel grimaced, but then smoothed out his expression before John noticed.

"Mom and Dad aren't here right now," Gabriel said. I barely knew him, but even I could sense something off in his clipped tone. "Rest a bit more while Arden gets herself together, and I'll fill you in over lunch. Just relax for now."

He rushed out of the room on the pretext of heating up the food, and John shot me a worried glance, signaling that something didn't seem right to him either.

"I'll be quick," I said. "I'd put it off until after lunch, but I'm kind of a mess."

I remembered Blue Hat getting blown off me, and the fine sheen of blood and gore that had misted over me, and clutched my arms around myself to hide my shudder. The memory made me feel hollow—not hollow exactly, but like all the good things inside me had been scraped away, replaced with dark shadows where awful things hid from the light. I had never known anyone who died. That my first encounter was so traumatizing, and that the dead were men who'd been trying to hurt me, was seriously fucking with my head. The more I tried to push the images away, the more they sprang to the forefront of my mind. John's blood, Blue Hat's blood, his weight on top of me...

My heart was racing and my palms felt sweaty, even though I logically knew I was safe now. My breathing was out of sync and out of my control. My distress must have been apparent because John grabbed my hand, anchoring me to the present.

"Maggie told me what happened to us. Well, what Gabriel saw when he got there, and how...how he saved us. How you tried to. I don't remember any of it, but I know you do," he said. His eyes shone with concern. "Don't think you have to keep it to yourself just because everything else is going to hell."

I thought of John sprawled in the snow. Of the incredible loudness of the gunshot in the still woods, and the fact that Gabriel had killed two men without even blinking and he would hate me forever because of it.

"Thanks, but I think I'd rather try to forget at the moment. Some good old repression sounds right up my alley right about now." I stepped into the dim, unfamiliar hallway and headed to the bathroom.

"Try getting hit in the head with a giant rock," John called after me. "It's much more effective than booze ever was."

3

I walked into the bathroom and nearly turned to leave when I saw someone inside.

"Wait! I was just running your bath for you," Maggie said. She turned off the water and stood to her full height—much taller than me—wiping her hands off on her jeans before extending one in my direction. "It's nice to finally meet you, Arden. I mean, I wish it was under different circumstances, but what are you gonna do?"

I took her hand, and we shared a shrug and a smile. After a misguided attempt at substitute teaching in high schools, I found teenagers repellent in general, but Maggie seemed okay so far.

"Thanks for the bath," I said. "I'll try to be quick."

"No prob. I just wanted to make sure you weren't shy about using the hot water. Gabriel can be such a dictator about it. We don't have 'hard-ass Asian parents,'" she said, curling her index and middle fingers into air quotes, "but Gabriel somehow developed the first-born-male-must-be-stoic-and-honor-family trait. He can be such a stereotype sometimes."

I wanted to join in on the brother-bashing, but the guy had just saved my life, so I couldn't be too hard on him. "Well, he's a lot older than you. Maybe he had it a little tougher than you did." When she looked hurt at my defense of him, I added, "Or maybe he just has a stick up his ass. That stick doesn't discriminate by race, gender or class, kid."

She giggled, her large brown eyes shining at me. She was pretty nice for a sixteen-year-old.

"Anyway, there's soap, shampoo, a razor...but I put some Epsom salt in the water, so you might want to avoid shaving just yet," she said, holding up a blue cardboard carton and shaking it. "It's supposed to help when you're sore, but I don't think it would feel too awesome if you cut yourself."

Okay, she was more than nice; she was an angel.

My body hurt like hell, especially my jaw. Despite being a grade-A asshole at times, I'd never been hit before and I was shocked at how much my face hurt in the aftermath. It was a dull, throbbing pain that flashed into brilliance when I pressed at the point of impact, which I couldn't seem to stop doing due to some previously unknown masochistic streak. Blue Hat had possessed a mean right hook, but he wouldn't get another chance to use it.

"I scrounged up an outfit for you," Maggie said, pointing to a shirt and pants draped on the sink. "They're a bit big since you're the size of, like, a munchkin, but we donated most of the clothes from before my growth spurt."

"Thanks," I said, my voice quavering. I'd been so busy worrying about John and sparring with Gabriel that I hadn't allowed myself to truly understand I was someplace safe, where baths and fresh clothes were an option. When we'd set out on our journey, driven from our home by hunger and uncertainty, we'd convinced ourselves it would be easy. We had been wrong. At various points during the trek, I'd wanted to collapse in the snow and give up. Sleepless nights, mindless fear, being attacked—after all that, a simple act of kindness from a teenager threatened to reduce me to tears.

"No problem. Let me know if you need anything else." She made a quick retreat from the bathroom, closing the door to give me privacy.

I grunted another thanks at the closed door before peeling my smelly clothes off. Now that I was in a setting that was clean and comfortable, the level of filth that had somehow become normal reverted back to what it really was—horrific. The enormity of what John and I had experienced set in when I looked at the pile of filthy clothing on the bathroom floor. Weeks ago, I would have considered wearing the same blouse twice as something reserved for extreme measures; the white T-shirt I'd just shucked off had been sweated through so many times that it'd turned yellow.

My, how things changed when the world stopped spinning.

I glanced at the full-length mirror and was shocked to see how much my body had altered. My skin, which usually had a healthy mocha glow, was ashy and gray. My body, which had once brought all the boys to the yard, was unhealthily thin, and my hair was more like a brittle rat's nest than I'd realized when I'd joked with John. Dark smudges under my eyes segued into the bruise blossoming across my cheek.

"Jesus," I whispered, closing my eyes against my reflection. It was painful enough that I didn't look like myself, but worse that I wasn't entirely unrecognizable. For a second, I'd seen my mom when she was at her sickest, staring back at me.

For the briefest moment, the desire to leave and go to my parents by any means blotted out all other thought, but it was quickly crushed by the hopeless reality of logistics. My parents lived in Northern California, which may as well have been another planet, given our current situation.

If I was this beat-up after traveling a hundred miles, trying to travel thousands would be enacting a death wish.

It was impossible for me to think of their advanced age and health problems—and the fact that I wasn't there to protect them—without imagining the worst. A crushing helplessness pressed down on me, clouding my brain and sending tendrils of panic down my spine. I took a deep, shuddering breath. I couldn't think of my parents and their well-being right now without risking my sanity. If I was going to have a mental breakdown, it would be slightly less mortifying if I weren't naked to boot. I turned away from the mirror on shaky legs and sought the heated refuge of the bathtub.

Instead of worrying myself into an anxiety attack, I tried to focus on the positive aspects of walking nearly one hundred miles in a few days. *My leg muscles are more defined. I got to commune with nature and sleep under the stars. I discovered that maple leaves are softer than that cheap toilet paper John always buys.*

The hot water slipped over my body and my muscles began to unclench. I hadn't even realized they were so tight. I could feel the weeks of tension and fear, and days of hiking and hiding and constant vigilance, seeping from my body while the heat soaked into me. I used the rose-scented bodywash next to the tub, scrubbing at my skin as if I could wash away the memories of the past weeks too.

I tried to take advantage of the opportunity to condition and detangle my hair, but my shoulders and neck screamed with pain as I tried to work out the knots. I was injured worse than I'd realized.

It may be time for that big chop, I thought viciously. I managed to comb through the tangled mess, contorting myself into strange positions to get at my hair without wrenching my shoulders, but I eventually had to give up, unable to deal with the pain.

I soaped up one more time, although the water was already murky; who knew when I'd have another hot bath? We had the generator, but I'd learned that creature comforts could be snatched away from you in an instant. I tried to massage my calves and thighs as I soaped them, but even my hands were sore, scraped and abraded from clawing at the iced-over snow while trying to break free from Blue Hat.

What I really need is a masseuse with big, strong hands. A vision of Gabriel's hands popped into my head, large and long-fingered as they wound John's bandages.

Nope, not going there. Ain't nobody got time for that. Despite my internal protests, I already knew what his fingers felt like against my skin. My traitorous mind supplied the sensation of his hands against my face, and then my imagination took it further. I could almost feel his fingertips trailing along the sensitive skin of my neck, moving across my shoulders to my chest and down farther than any appropriate massage should go...

Although the water had cooled, I was suddenly warm and my shoulders were no longer the only part of my body that was throbbing.

"This is ridiculous," I grumbled, standing so abruptly that I sloshed filthy bathwater onto the floor.

I dried off and put on the thick black leggings and soft gray sweatshirt, indeed too big but comfortable nonetheless, that Maggie had laid out for me. I pulled my hair back into a bun—I'd deal with that mess later, when it didn't feel as if someone was cleaving at my shoulder blades every time I raised my arms.

I was finally feeling halfway human again. A clean bra would've been nice, of course, but beggars couldn't be choosers. I washed mine out by hand.

After cleaning the bathtub to the best of my ability, I headed back to the bedroom to drop my stuff off.

Gabriel sat on the edge of the bed I'd been sleeping on. His elbows were on his knees and his face rested in his steepled fingers as he gazed at John, who was dozing. His brow was furrowed and half his face was hidden by his hands, but I had to admit that he was far from gross despite what I wanted to believe. Like many a jerk I had known, he was quite handsome.

I must've made a sound because his head turned in

my direction. His eyes were large and expressive, and the despair I saw in them shook me. It was the same desolate look that stared out from the TV screen in those Save the Children commercials I hated for messing with my emotions. Before I could blink, his expression shuttered and he was back to being the self-assured older brother with an attitude.

"I cleaned the bathtub," I said to deflect from the fact that I'd been caught staring.

"Good. You're going to be expected to contribute however you can while you're here."

He was much more attractive when he wasn't speaking.

"No shit, Sherlock. Hence, the cleaning of the bathtub," I said. "I'm fully capable of pulling my weight."

He gave a curt nod in reply and got up to leave the room. "Wake up John when you're done. We'll be ready to eat pretty soon."

When he walked past me he was so close that I could feel the heat coming off his body in the cool air. He smelled of sweat, but not in a bad way—rather, in a way that was virile and pleasing. I'd always scoffed at women who insisted the scent of a man's sweat was attractive, but the spiral of desire that uncurled in my belly undercut my disdain.

"Okay," I said testily. I crossed my arms over my chest, annoyed both at him and myself. And then I remembered my manners. "Thank you, by the way."

"For what?"

"For saving my life. For...stopping those guys."

He looked down quickly, angrily. "I heard you yell," he said. "I saw John lying there and I didn't even think. After that it's just a blur. But I killed two men."

His gaze locked to mine, and what I saw there made me wish he'd kept his head down. The inappropriate sexual tension I'd been experiencing fizzled immediately at the sight of the desolation in his eyes, and rightly so. I didn't know if the world was ending or even if my family was still alive, and here I was getting the warm fuzzies about John's jerky brother.

"You did it to save John. And his dumb roommate. I can't imagine how you must feel," I said, my hand instinctively reaching for his arm. My fingertips only grazed him before he pulled away from me.

"No, you can't. Hopefully, you'll never be able to. But let's get one thing straight. I wouldn't have had to kill those men if you hadn't led John off course. If you do anything even remotely as stupid as that again, you're out of here and I don't care what John has to say about it. My priority is to protect my family until this mess is over, got that?"

He whirled and stalked away, not bothering to wait for an answer.

"Got it," I said to his retreating form. My throat nearly closed up and tears burned my eyes, but I blinked them back and released a shaky breath.

I was glad we'd made it to this place, but I had no idea how to move forward without messing things up. Everything I did seemed to annoy Gabriel. Did he really dislike me enough to force me out into the unknown? Just the thought of having to go back outside, out where there were more people who would try to hurt me, filled me with dread. My chest felt heavy, as if Blue Hat was still sitting there leering down at me, as if he would always be there.

I heard a rustle of sheets before John jumped to his feet beside me.

"That's enough," he said, his voice going up an octave. His dark eyes were wide and his nostrils flared—it was the angriest I'd ever seen him. That was saying a lot, considering I'd been there when he'd discovered his ex, Peter, had been banging his way through the University of Rochester athletics department.

"No, he's right," I said, trying to grab a hold of him as he stormed past me. He would have been adorable, dressed in mismatched pajamas with his hair sticking out from the bandage at crazy angles, if he hadn't been so gloriously pissed off.

"Gabriel!" John called out. I heard Gabriel's jogging steps and a moment later he was back in the room, eyes wide with worry.

"What's wrong?" Gabriel asked, reaching toward John's head.

John ducked under his arm, his injury not slowing down his reflexes. "You need to let this go right now." His back was ramrod straight as he stared up at his brother. "I'm not going to let you make Arden feel like shit for no reason."

"No reason? What are you talking about? I have blood on my hands because she had a tantrum," he spat. For just a second, Gabriel's authoritative asshole routine slipped away and I saw anguish and anger in his eyes. That look pierced me more than any of his words had. If it had been the other way around—if I thought Gabriel had nearly gotten John killed, and that he had forced my hand so I had to kill others—would I be able to forgive him at the drop of a hat? Not fucking likely.

John stepped close to Gabriel and stared up into his face, eyes flashing. "You have blood on your hands because of *me*," he said. "I was leading us here, I knew we were close and I thought it would be fine to let her practice her navigating. To be honest, I was delaying because I was scared of what I'd find when we got here. I let Arden think she browbeat me, but I didn't have to give in to her. So what happened was my fault. My concussion—my fault. All that bruising on Arden's face—my fault. What you had to do to those men—*my fault*."

John was nearly yelling into Gabriel's face by this point, but the older brother didn't flinch. He simply gazed at John and nodded, as though he was turning the words over in his mind.

"Okay," Gabriel said. He clamped one hand on the door frame and gave a final sharp nod. "Okay. I'm sorry. I was taking out my frustrations on Arden. I overreacted and I was wrong."

I was shocked that he gave in so easily, but then I remembered the adoration he had bestowed on John earlier. He would apologize to appease him, even if he didn't mean it.

John sighed, his body sagging as the fight left him. "No, you aren't *wrong*, just..." He shook his head, struggling for the right words. "You don't always have to be so intense about everything. You saved my life yesterday, and it's not like it's the first time. You had to kill, when you've taken an oath to protect life. It's normal to be angry. You would be a sociopath if you weren't upset. But direct the anger at the right person."

John clasped Gabriel's shoulders and leaned forward, his face softening while they shared some kind of sibling bonding moment I couldn't even begin to speculate on, as an only child.

John quirked a brow. "I'm all beat-up. I mean, I got hit in the head with a *rock*. A big one! You can't stay mad at me for too long, can you?"

I couldn't believe it when John's supremely effective puppy dog face got Gabriel to crack a smile. He looked like a totally different person. Unfortunately for me, that person was even more attractive than the brooding version of the man. A deep dimple on his left cheek and straight white teeth that pressed into his lower lip, emphasizing its plumpness. He had a tractor beam smile, one that pulled you into his orbit whether you wanted to go or not; I wouldn't have put up much resistance.

There really is something wrong with me. I tore my eyes away from Gabriel's endearing grin before I pictured us holding hands and skipping through a meadow, or something equally mortifying.

"Let's go downstairs," Gabriel said. "And don't try that face on Maggie to beg for more food. She's just as immune to it as Mom is."

"Try what?" John asked, poking out his bottom lip. He threaded his arm through Gabriel's, leaning on him as they walked. His outburst had taken a lot out of him and he probably should have gone back to bed, but he still turned to me and winked, as if everything would be all right.

I followed, wishing I hadn't seen Gabriel's stricken expression earlier. If I hadn't, I might have been able to wink back.

4

Gabriel and John headed toward what I assumed was the kitchen, judging from the delicious smells coming from that direction. My stomach cramped painfully. Running out of food was one of the things that had driven us from our condo to this cabin. A giant bag of peanuts that we'd purchased from Costco on a whim had actually ended up being our saving grace. On our trek over, most of our meals had consisted of handfuls of nuts. It wasn't the most filling thing, but it had provided us with plenty of protein on our long trek up here.

Maggie was setting candles around the long wooden table in the dining alcove when I walked in. The space was already lit by the flickering of two huge candles that sat on opposite sides of the room like waxy toadstools.

"I always wondered who bought these giant candles,"

I said, nudging one with my sock-clad foot as I walked by. "Now I see they really can come in handy."

"My mom went nuts at a candle outlet a few years back and filled the back of their van with these things. My dad said it was a waste of money. Little did he know..."

Her voice trailed off and she turned, her face hidden by her dark sheet of hair. My stomach dropped. Whatever they had to tell John about his parents, it wasn't good. I hoped I was misreading something though. It was bad enough that I wouldn't know what happened to my parents until this crisis passed and electricity was restored. That John and his siblings should suffer, too, was doubly unfair.

I heard a quiet sniffle before she turned back to me, eyes glossy with tears she'd blinked away. She seemed so young and defenseless in that moment that I wanted to hug her, but she shrugged and slid her disaffected teen mask back into place before setting a few tea candles around.

"We have the generator, but we don't know how long whatever is happening is going to last," she continued. "So it makes sense to conserve diesel. We don't need too much light. Most nights we read or play board games in the living room, where the fireplace is. I practice guitar sometimes, but I think I'm dangerously close to pushing Gabriel over the edge."

"He doesn't like music?" I asked. I could totally imagine him being the kind of repressed weirdo who thought music was for slackers.

"No, it's that I can't really play," she said with a shy

smile. "I'd started taking lessons, but I didn't have a chance to learn more than a few songs."

"Well, I play guitar," I said. "I'm no Eric Clapton, but I can teach you a song or two if you want to continue your lessons."

Maggie nearly dropped the tray of candles in her rush to cross the room to me. "Really? That would be so great, Arden!" she said, grabbing my arms and jumping with excitement. I couldn't hide my yelp of pain as her movements rocked my aching shoulders. "Oh my God, I'm sorry! Are you okay? Are you hurt?"

John walked into the room, carrying a pitcher of water. "What are you squealing about? Arden, I hope you're not already corrupting my innocent sister with your wanton ways."

Gabriel followed close at his heels carrying a large, steaming pot.

Maggie shook her head. "She just volunteered to teach me guitar, and I got all excited and ended up hurting her."

"What's wrong?" John and Gabriel asked in unison, and I shook my head, even though my shoulders and back were killing me. I was already imposing on this family enough. I didn't need them going out of their way for me, especially seeing how Gabriel was the resident medic. The pain would go away eventually, and it was certainly easier to deal with than he was.

"I'm fine, just a little strain." I rolled my shoulders to show them I was okay, gritting my teeth against the stabbing sensation that radiated through my back.

Gabriel studied me as he approached with the heavy pot. "Good. Can you carry this to the table then? I'm going to go get the rice."

He met my eyes in challenge, holding the huge pot out to me. I reached forward to take it, staring back at him. My hands closed over his on the handles of the pot, and he let me bear its weight for just a second before raising his eyebrows at me.

"It's pretty heavy," he said, and I saw something like mirth flash in his amber eyes. He was enjoying fucking with me.

I closed my eyes and took a deep breath to calm myself. I knew it was petty to hold a grudge against someone who was allowing me to shelter in his family's home and giving me access to food and water and heat; regardless of what a bastard-coated bastard he'd been to me, I was indebted to him, and to John and Maggie. Gabriel had apologized, and now we were supposed to be playing at one-big-happy, so kicking him in the shin wouldn't help the situation. Anyway, with my luck I'd end up accidentally breaking his leg and wouldn't even be able to savor the moment.

"Okay, I may have pulled something when I was fighting with Tweedledee and Tweedledum yesterday," I admitted, releasing my hold on the pot. "I'll be fine but I can't carry this right now, unless you want to lick your food up from the floor."

"I'll check you out after we eat," Gabriel said, satisfied with my acquiescence. He set the pot in the middle of the table.

"Thanks, but that isn't necessary." I tried to keep the edge of annoyance out of my voice.

"Oh, I wasn't making a suggestion." He walked back toward the kitchen, as if that was the end of the discussion.

"Really, it's okay," I called out. Why was he pushing this? I just wanted to eat whatever was the source of the delicious smell, and then to be left alone.

Gabriel gave an annoyed sigh as he returned, placing a large bowl of rice on the table. "Look, we need to make sure that if any of us is injured, we take care of the problem right away. That's better than having a minor injury turn into a big deal later, isn't it? Besides, it's my job. I'm not trying to cop a feel or anything."

I gave a sharp nod to end the conversation and decided not to acknowledge that comment, or the sting of embarrassment that he didn't *want* to cop a feel and was fine with announcing it to everyone. I sealed my lips and set out bowls and utensils at the place settings.

The meal, a simple but hearty stew of kimchi and vegetables served over a heaping helping of rice, was the most delicious thing I'd ever eaten. I focused on grabbing clumps of food with my chopsticks, on the textured tang of the kimchi and the perfectly tender grains of rice. After a diet of pantry leavings and peanuts, I'd forgotten the hedonistic pleasure that a good meal could provide.

"This is so good," I breathed, resisting the urge to drop the fancy chopsticks we were using and shovel the food into my mouth with my hands.

"Thanks," Gabriel said, surprising me. Despite my strident feminism, I'd assumed Maggie had made the tasty meal.

"Gabriel does everything around here," Maggie said with the slightest trace of resentment in her tone. It was gone when she continued, and I wondered if I was simply searching for an ally to join me on Team Gabriel Sucks. "I'm glad you like kimchi though. Mom has jars and jars of it downstairs. And pickles. And jams. She and Dad have been really into canning lately, especially since they expanded the garden last summer."

I thought of my parents' lush backyard garden. They'd discovered the hard way that two green thumbs didn't necessarily produce a natural-born gardener; I'd killed every plant they'd ever entrusted to me. They should have taken that as some kind of statement on my character, but they loved me enough to overlook it.

"We have plenty of other stuff," Gabriel said. "There's pretty much the entire inventory of a grocery store shoved down there in addition to the homemade stuff."

"Their canned food is better," Maggie said with unnecessary harshness. I sensed a hint of the wobble that had affected her voice earlier, and now that we were all seated, the cause of her distress became evident. The two empty chairs at each end of the table were hard to ignore, although

Gabriel appeared to be trying mightily to do just that.

"Where *are* Mom and Dad?" John asked in a voice that aimed for casual but was laced with worry.

"Don't eat too much, John and Arden," Gabriel said as if he hadn't heard the question. "Your stomachs might not be able to handle rich food right away."

He shoveled some food into his mouth and chewed for a long time, so long that I wondered whether anything was left or he was faking it. It was then that I remembered how frightened he'd looked when he'd first bent over John, and the words he'd spoken aloud.

I can't lose you too.

Fuck. I steeled myself against whatever bombshell he was about to drop.

Gabriel finally swallowed, spun his chopsticks between two long fingers and then slapped them onto the table. "Mom and Dad went missing about a week ago," he said bluntly, talking over John's stunned gasp. "I got back into town right before everyone started locking themselves away, when people were still being optimistic about what might be going on. After a couple of weeks of the store being closed, we decided to take all the stock that hadn't gone bad and move it here. They gave the neighbors some food and supplies, too, but we moved the bulk of it in the van and decided this would be the safest place to wait things out."

He picked up the chopsticks and took another bite of his dinner, chewing mechanically as if eating was the last thing he wanted to be doing. For a moment, I was annoyed on John's behalf—he deserved to know more than that. Then I realized Gabriel probably wasn't capable of saying more, not without losing his cool.

Maggie took over for him. "They decided to go check on Darlene, who lives out in the boonies," she said. I wondered what could be boonier than our current location but kept my questions to myself. "She's been working in the store for the last year or so. I told them not to go, but she's pregnant and her husband is stationed in Iraq. They said it was the right thing to do." Tears welled up in her eyes again, but this time she couldn't hide them and they rolled down her cheeks in fat droplets. "They didn't come back, John. We don't know where they are," she whispered.

My heart ached for John, and for Gabriel and Maggie too. That hollow feeling inside me echoed with the knowledge that we were a house full of orphans now, possibly forever if this crisis didn't end soon. An undefinable heaviness descended on me at the thought that I'd never get to show my mom that I'd mastered her vegetable lasagna, or play the latest songs I'd learned on guitar for my dad, who'd taught me the basics. That I'd never smell that combination of lemony pine cleaner and cologne that hit me every time I walked in the front door of the house I'd grown up in. The weight that I felt, that all of us felt, was the knowledge that we might never see our parents again. It was an idea so immense that it had become tangible. I bit my lip against the pressure behind my eyes.

I know John was upset that they'd waited to tell him,

but I understood. Having their brother show up must have been like a miracle for them, despite his injury, and who would want to spoil that with a dose of terrible reality?

"Do you think they decided to stay someplace else?" John asked in a voice that only trembled a bit. I could tell by the way he scratched at the side of his nose that he was trying to hide how incredibly upset he was. When you lived with someone long enough, you started to learn his tells. "They could just be holed up somewhere."

"They would have tried to contact us," Gabriel said. "They took a walkie-talkie with them."

"Maybe they don't work where they are," John said calmly. "I don't know about here, but we weren't able to get anything on our radio but static. There's definitely something, or someone, messing with radio waves. Maybe the interference is what's making it impossible for them to get in touch."

Maggie sniffled and wiped at her eyes. "Maybe," she said. She picked up her spoon and took a small bite of food.

I sat watching the whole thing silently, not knowing what I could say that wouldn't make things worse. *Hey, I have no idea if my parents are alive either! High five!* I spooned more food into my bowl and stuffed my face. That was easier than thinking of John's possibly dead parents, or worse, my own. Trying to ignore the fear was easier said than done—my food could barely eke past the lump in my throat as images of my parents fighting off home invaders or slowly starving to death flashed before my eyes.

No. They're okay. They have to be okay.

"They'll be back," John said. "I mean, Dad taught me everything I know, and I made it here. And Mom would cut any fool who messes with Dad. Remember when that idiot tried to rob the store?"

Gabriel chuckled and nodded.

"He ended up with two black eyes and a broken arm," Gabriel said with a look in my direction. Everyone else already knew the story. "Mom didn't have a scratch on her."

"She's tough," Maggie said with conviction. "Like you, Arden. She wouldn't go down without a fight, either."

I managed a smile, but it was hard thinking of my parents, who were the opposite of tough. They'd had me late in life. They were old and trusting and always trying to help someone, even though my mother had plenty of problems of her own.

I pushed them out of my mind. I could only hope that because they were good people, someone had taken care of them when everything went down and they hadn't been left to the wiles of strangers.

They wouldn't have to depend on strangers if you were there. The thought was like a sharp, unexpected kick to the solar plexus, and it was entirely true.

"I don't know about you, but I'm glad not to be eating peanuts anymore," John said, pulling me back into the conversation and changing the topic in one fell swoop. He reached down and gave my hand a squeeze, and I returned it. I didn't know if my face had betrayed my distress or if he only thought of his own need for comfort, but I was grateful. He didn't let go of me; we just continued to eat, taking succor where we could find it.

"Ugh, never say the P-word word in my presence again," I said, shifting to ease the pull of John's weight on my arm and shoulder. "It's to be referred to as 'The Legume That Shall Not Be Named' from this point forward."

"What are you talking about?" Maggie asked, keeping her eyes studiously away from our entwined hands, as if our childlike behavior embarrassed her.

Gabriel raised his brows but said nothing.

John filled her in on the diet of necessity we had undertaken when we made our trek. I had known it was bad, but seeing Maggie's horrified expression really hit it home. They had been relatively safe and secure in this place, with plenty of food. Thoughts of starvation hadn't arrived here yet, although they would if this situation was never explained or resolved.

"That's seriously messed up," she said, gazing at the plate of food she'd been picking at. She ran her fingers through her bangs, shifting the hair so that it hid her eyes. "You guys didn't see anything when you were heading here? I mean, anything that could explain what's going on?"

"We tried to avoid contact with people on our way here," I said. "One of the reasons we left Rochester is that people were starting to lose it. Like, *Lord of the Flies* meets *The Hunger Games* losing it. At first everyone pulled together."

"We had winter cookouts with our neighbors," John added. "Lots of people shared their food that would've spoiled if it was left in the fridge. There were ice cream sundaes, and Arden's old boss gave out cases of beer that were going to skunk anyway... It was kind of fun."

I nodded. The first couple of days had been fun, our fears hidden by too much beer and jokes about toilets that wouldn't flush. I picked up where John had left off. "When FEMA never showed and supplies started to dwindle, so did the good vibes. A curfew was put in place after looters took to the streets, but the police were too busy trying to figure out what the hell was going on or protecting their own families to really bother enforcing it. A mosque a few blocks down was the first of the fires. Only a few people outside the congregation helped them, but there wasn't much anyone could do since there was no water. When the Russian restaurant down the street went up in flames, I couldn't tell whether the crowd was trying to snuff it out or adding fuel."

Mrs. Donskoy, a round and ruddy woman, had been one of my first customers when I'd decided to start freelancing as a bookkeeper. She'd give me cheese blintzes and, when it was blustery, a shot of vodka. I wondered where she was now.

"Oh my God. That's like something from a movie," Maggie whispered. "Everyone here just bought more ammo and stopped going outside much. There was no looting, but Mrs. Coleman did get mad when Mom and Dad decided to close up shop. They gave her a few free bags of chewing tobacco, and she went on her merry way."

I realized Maggie probably hadn't been exposed to anything truly violent, since they were in the middle of nowhere. One of the benefits of a sparsely populated area was there were fewer people to turn on you when the shit hit the fan, although Blue Hat and his friend had proven there was always an exception to the rule.

"It was real, unfortunately, although we did run into a few people along the way who were safe to talk to," John said, pointing a chopstick emphatically. "Not everyone has gone mad. None of them knew any more than we did though. Power outage, no TV signal, no radio transmissions, no explanation. In my informal poll, it was a toss-up between the Russians and space aliens."

"If it was the Russians, they must have developed a nuke that can go off without any mushroom cloud," I said.

"And no casualties," Gabriel added. "At least none who came to my ER."

I tried to imagine Gabriel in the chaos of an emergency room flooded with victims of some large-scale attack and shuddered. I had seen him in action and knew he could handle difficult situations, but it was still strange to think of him having responsibility over anyone's life. The stress of that was enough to make anyone an asshole, I imagined. Which came first, the asshole or the ER doc?

"Maybe it was an EMP," John said. When we all stared at him, he rolled his eyes and continued. "You know, an electromagnetic pulse? There's been talk of weaponizing the technology for years, and maybe that's what knocked out all the electricity. I mean, our atmosphere is littered with Russian satellites, so it wouldn't be that hard."

I sometimes forgot that beneath his fashionista exterior, John was a huge nerd, and a tech nerd at that. Probably because I usually zoned out whenever he started rambling about microprocessors and other technical gobbledygook.

"Or maybe it was the Canadians," I said before he could chime in with any additional terrifying possibilities. "I've been saying for years that they were trying to lull us into complacency with their 'friendly neighbors to the north' shtick. They're probably rolling in on their armored polar bears as we speak."

Gabriel looked at me as if I'd grown a second head, but John gave my hand another reassuring squeeze. Like I said, you lived with someone long enough and you started to learn her tells.

"Did you see any police or military? Any checkpoints or anything?" Gabriel asked, ignoring my Canuck conspiracy theory.

"No," John said. "We tried to stay away from the roads and hid when we heard engines. We weren't taking any chances. Or we thought we weren't."

His hand went clammy in mine before he gently

tugged it away and moved it to his head. It was still terrifying to think that a brain as unique and wonderful as his had nearly been smashed in. I hated that we couldn't trundle him off to a hospital to see if he was really okay. Like with everything else, we'd just have to wait and see.

"Damn," Gabriel's low voice bit out. "I was hoping you two knew something we didn't. This just doesn't make sense."

He shook his head, his face clouded by annoyance. Not knowing why the world had stopped working sucked for a regular person, but it was probably even worse for a control freak like him.

"What about the aurora borealis?" Maggie asked. "I mean, we're kind of far up, but that's not normal at all, and it's super freaky. Did you sleep outside under that? Do you think it's radiation, like from a nuke?"

I had no idea what the blazing aurora meant. It was beautiful, but a menacing beauty, like the flight of a thousand birds before a catastrophe strikes.

"We had a tent," I said. "Not that it would protect us from radiation any more than this house would. We ditched it at our last resting point since we thought we wouldn't need it anymore."

I was wondering if we would come to regret that decision. We had put this place up on a pedestal while we traveled. At the cabin, we would be warm and safe and well fed. His parents would be annoying but lovable, his siblings ready to welcome us with open arms. Nothing bad would happen to us there, so we wouldn't have to worry about leaving. Missing parents and dangerous mountain men hadn't been in the realm of possibilities.

We finished the meal in silence, each of us lost in thought. John and I hadn't learned anything new. We had come all this way searching for safety, but we'd been in search of answers too. The fact that we were still at square one made the reality of the situation even scarier. My heart started to beat little faster as panic welled up within me.

"I'm going to do the dishes," I said abruptly, pushing my chair away from the table. Cleaning helped clear my mind, especially dish duty. There was something soothing about the sudsy water and the scraping of ceramic that made me feel I was bringing order out of chaos.

"Don't be silly," Maggie said. "You need to let Gabriel check you out. I'll do them."

"You've already done so much today," I said, exasperated. "I want to help."

"You'll be able to help once we know you aren't hurt," Gabriel said, that air of command in his voice again. "You aren't going to be very useful if you can't carry anything, so let's just deal with this. Come to the living room. It's warmer there."

Gabriel left the room, and John stood and batted at the bun on my head. "I'll help Maggie," he said.

"But you're the one who's really hurt!" I protested.

"And I let Gabriel check me out and decide what I was capable of doing, because that's what's best for everyone." The saccharine and STFU was directed my way now.

I narrowed my eyes at him. I thought he'd understand my reticence, but he seemed to think that his little come-to-Jesus talk with Gabriel meant everything was okay now. It really was annoying that he was always right, though—it would be much easier to submit to Gabriel's exam than to make a scene and annoy everyone.

"Okay," I said. "But I get to do the dishes next time."

"Deal," Maggie said.

"Don't look so put out," John said as I walked past him. "You might even like it."

5

"All right, come sit over here," Gabriel said when I stepped into the living room. He sat on a battered recliner. A fire burned low in the hearth, and flickering shadows highlighted the sharp angles of his face as he leaned forward to pat the ottoman in front of him. Now that we were alone and he wasn't being an asshole for a minute, it was hard to focus on anything but the beauty of his features.

"I'm fine. Really," I said, suddenly shy. It wasn't as if I hadn't been between a man's legs before, and in more compromising positions than this, but I could already feel the flush rising to my cheeks at the thought of being so close to him.

Gabriel leaned his head against the sofa back and heaved a long, exaggerated sigh. "I'm a doctor," he said. "I promise not to manhandle you."

Let's not rule anything out just yet, the unhelpful part of my brain whispered as I settled onto the ottoman. His hands brushed against my shoulders, and I jumped at the contact even though I had expected it. He pulled away.

"Did that hurt?" he asked, real concern in his voice.

I shook my head. "You just caught me off guard."

"Sorry. Guess my bedside manner is getting rusty. I'm going to palpate the area around your back and shoulders to make sure you haven't torn anything. Okay?"

I gave a nod, and then his hands were on me, prodding and poking at my shoulders, all the while explaining what he was doing and asking me questions in that deep, reassuring tone of his.

This guy is the Barry White of doctors, I thought as he rotated my shoulder while instructing me on the pain scale and asking what my injury rated. There was no earthly reason for him to both be totally hot *and* have a voice that made my panties start creeping down of their own accord. I wasn't even wearing any, and they were already halfway to my ankles.

Maybe it was because my back was to him and I couldn't tell if he was glaring at me or had really meant his apology, but his hands felt good and the way he spoke to me, knowledgeable and professional, made me feel safer than I had since this whole ordeal had begun.

Don't go getting Stockholm syndrome now, I thought, but brushed it away to focus on the feeling of security, something I knew would be fleeting. Besides, Gabriel wasn't holding me captive; he had saved me. And now he was tending to me. Jerkiness aside, he'd done more for me in two days than most of the men I'd ever dated. I didn't know if that spoke more to his character, or mine.

"Looks like you've just strained some muscles," he said, interrupting the tumult of my thoughts. "I don't think anything is torn, judging from the fact that you weren't screaming in agony while I examined you."

"Well, that's good," I said. "I don't like feeling useless."

"Same here. I'm going to get something to ease your pain," he said. I felt him stand, and then the reassuring presence of his weight behind me was gone. I didn't like the sudden coolness at my back, so I stood to snoop around the place I'd be calling home until everything went back to normal.

If it ever went back to normal.

I paced the room, with its shabby chic furniture and well-worn rug, glancing at the pictures of John's family lining the mantelpiece. The smaller frames displayed the siblings at various stages of development: John, thin and fine-boned, as he still was, and Gabriel, surprisingly roly-poly given his currently chiseled body. One picture featured a toddling Maggie chasing after her brothers, who ran through a pile of leaves in the front yard. The largest picture, hung over the fireplace, showed their parents on their wedding day.

Instead of a white dress, their mother wore what appeared to be a silk robe, but on closer inspection appeared to be a separate jacket and skirt. The fabric was a vibrant red, and both sleeves and skirt belled out. Her shiny black hair was pulled into a front knot adorned with flowers and golden hairpins, and her fine-featured face was porcelain pale except for her bright red lips. Mr. Seong was shorter than his wife. He wore a royal blue robe, similar in style to Mrs. Seong's outfit. A rounded black hat sat atop his head, emphasizing the sweet boyishness of his face. They held hands in front of a flowering cherry blossom tree, smiling radiantly. Although they faced forward, their gazes were tilted toward each other.

Gabriel's footsteps sounded behind me and I whirled to face him, feeling as if I'd been caught doing something inappropriate.

"Here. It's just ibuprofen," he said, his golden eyes avoiding the picture of his parents as he handed me two pills and a cup of water. "We have stronger stuff, but I think we should save it, just in case."

We'd already had one medical emergency, so his caution made sense

"Thanks," I said, downing the pills dry and then taking a sip. I pointed to the picture of him and John. "You were a cute kid."

"I was a chubby kid," he grumbled, his hand darting out to lay the incriminating picture frame flat before continuing. "That picture was taken during what I like to call 'the

Nutella period.' When your parents own a grocery store, you don't always make the healthiest decisions. I once broke into a case of the stuff and took a spoonful from each jar, thinking no one would notice. John tried to stop me, but I didn't listen because I was older and therefore smarter. Boy, was I wrong."

I cackled, imagining a small, round Gabriel methodically twisting open jars and spooning the delicious spread into his mouth, sure he'd come up with the perfect plan to avoid detection.

"What happened when you got caught?"

"My mom told me I could eat the whole case since I liked it so much. I think you can imagine how that played out."

"Is that in every mom's playbook?" I asked, empathizing. "I had a similar experience with a giant jar of pickles. Let's just say that after that day, relish was never a topping of choice for me."

We groaned out a laugh, and I wondered if we were both thinking the same thing: *Will I ever see my mom again?*

"Anyway, I have this salve that should help with the pain." He held out his hand to reveal a small container of Tiger Balm. "I don't think you'll be able to reach your shoulders and back without hurting yourself. I can apply it, if you want."

To my chagrin, the fantasy that had plagued me during my bath flashed in my head. Gabriel was offering to put his hands on my body, and given the way I suddenly tightened everywhere, my traitorous body was totally down with this plan. I realized that my only reply had been to simply gawk at him when he added, "Or I can get John to do it, or Maggie."

"You can do it," I blurted out, instantly regretting it as my body warmed. My nether regions were already stirring, suddenly interested in the events of the evening. "I mean, one of them can do it if you prefer, but you're a professional, right? You've probably had to do worse things than this."

"I'm a new doctor, but applying salve to your back would rank pretty low on the list of worst things I've had to do. One day I'll tell you about the woman who came into the ER with a bottle of soda lodged somewhere unfortunate." He paused, then raised his eyebrows. "A two-liter bottle."

"As delightful as that anecdote sounds, I'll pass, thanks."

We resumed our positions, him on the sofa and me on the ottoman. There was a silence and I realized he was trying to figure out how to go about applying the stuff.

"Should I just lift my shirt from behind?" I asked.

"Uh, yeah. Let me do it so you don't hurt yourself." He grabbed the back of the long sweatshirt and lifted it up and over my head. My arms were still in the sleeves, so the material bunched in the front, providing the perfect headrest for me while leaving my back completely exposed. It felt strangely intimate, revealing myself to him in this way. It was no more than he would have seen if I'd asked him to slap sunscreen on for me at the beach, but there was more at play here. Knowing that his gaze was fixed on my bare skin made my back prickle in anticipation of the touch that was soon to come.

He cleared his throat and shifted on the sofa. I wondered if I was radiating invisible perv waves that were making him uncomfortable.

"I hope you don't have cold hands," I said like a dork, hoping to break the tension that was now palpable. Well, I was pretty certain any tension in the air was emanating solely from me, but I had to at least put up a front of calm indifference.

"I've actually always been told the opposite," he said. "The patients during my ob-gyn rotation were especially grateful."

"Did you take a dose of overshare while you were grabbing the balm?" I asked, and then realized that he'd just cracked at least two jokes in a row that weren't at my expense. Great. Of course, he had to go and be funny on top of being fine.

I heard him unscrew the cap of the small jar, followed by the moist dip of his fingers into the salve. The sharp smells of camphor and menthol filled my nose, and then his hands were on my skin and, praise the Flying Spaghetti Monster, it was wonderful. His hands were indeed warm, but they were also skilled and gentle as they worked the balm into my aching muscles.

I'd thought he was just going to slather it on and send me on my way, but he took his time, applying it with the technique of a pro masseur. His thumbs slid firmly along the column of my neck, and it felt so good that I let out the beginnings of a moan. I stifled the remainder of the sound, embarrassed that the contact affected me so. He smoothed his hands over my shoulders, applying a bit more pressure each time. He did this again and again until my back felt warmed through, the clenched muscles loosening as he worked. Gabriel's palms were calloused, adding an extra layer of sensation to the massage, a friction that enhanced the already delicious heat of his hands against my skin.

He worked his way down, kneading at my back with both his knuckles and the balls of his palms. His fingers slid under the ridges of my shoulder blades, which I hadn't classified as an erogenous zone until that very moment. He dug in hard at first, and I cried out in pain, but as the knotted muscle broke down beneath his fingertips, the sharp torment faded and transformed into something edging on gratification.

He eased up. "Sorry. I can be a little rough sometimes, but once I work out these knots, you'll feel much better."

I bit back a whimper—I'd had massages before, and they'd felt damn good, but not like this. Even the painful kneading had strung garlands of excitement over my most sensitive parts. Gabriel's impromptu rubdown was loosening the taut muscles in my back, but other areas of my body were tightening in response, aching for the same attention.

As time stretched on, his hands began to move in a way that seemed exploratory rather than perfunctory. They glided slowly over each vertebra, as if there was some Braille message hidden in the indentation of bone and cartilage. They moved farther away from my shoulders, down to my lower back, which ached from days of walking and carrying a heavy pack. The pleasure of his touch built in such a way that it radiated from the point of contact, spreading over my skin in something akin to a ticklish sensation, except tickling didn't make me quiver and silently beg for more of the same. I squirmed between his legs and released a shuddering breath, momentarily unable to hide my reaction to this onslaught of sensation as he alternated between deep kneading and feathery caresses.

"Oh, right there," I blurted out when he began to work out a tight knot near the base of my spine. The exquisite combination of pain and pleasure Gabriel was inflicting on me was making it hard to keep quiet. My nipples hardened and pressed into the material of the sweatshirt, and I regretted not searching for a bra after my bath.

I willed myself to simply enjoy the comforting touch of another person, a professional person, but little by little the inappropriate thoughts began to rise, unbidden. Me slipping out of my shirt, Gabriel's hands on my arms turning me to face him, his mouth pressing against mine...

I felt like the ultimate perv—Gabriel was helping to ensure I wasn't in pain, and I repaid him by acting like the jerk who went to a spa and asked for a happy ending. Horrified by my inability to control the desire flashing within me,

I tried to think of anything that could stop the quickening of my pulse.

Bugs, baseball, cow dung, England—get a hold of yourself, woman!

"Did you pay your way through medical school by working as a masseuse, by any chance?" I asked. Maybe conversation could distract him from my rising temperature. The room was cool, but I felt as if I was sitting directly in the hearth and not in front of it. I knew my skin was hot to the touch. His touch.

He barked out a short, bassy laugh that resonated in my stomach and various other parts of my anatomy. "No, I tutored football players, but it's good to know I have an alternate career to fall back on," he said as his fingers worked their magic on me. "It's probably the Tiger Balm. People are addicted to this stuff. My parents swear by it."

In the weighted pause after his statement, I felt my heat cool down to a simmer, even though he continued massaging, moving his hands back to my shoulders and kneading the muscles there.

"They look so happy in their wedding photo," I said.

"They were happy people." The even rhythm of his hands jolted to a stop. "They *are* happy people." He paused, but then the frustration he'd been bottling up spilled out. "This is such bullshit. My parents came here and built themselves from the ground up. They gave us everything. And how did I repay them? I let them go out there by themselves. I should have been the one to make the delivery to Darlene. And since I didn't, I should have gone after them when they didn't come back."

I was surprised by his admission. Not by what he was saying—that part made sense. More by the fact that he'd opened up to me of all people. Then I remembered that I was the only one here who wasn't feeling the absence of his parents so acutely that talking about it would be unbearably painful.

"From everything I've heard, your parents are two competent adults who know how to take care of themselves," I said.

"I should have taken care of them," he replied, unmoved.

I tried a different tack. "Would you have left Maggie by herself to go look for them, not knowing for sure that John was going to show up?" I asked.

"No," he said, his voice a bit too sharp. "I just wish I knew they were okay."

I didn't say anything, but glanced at the picture of his parents from the corner of my eye. He resumed the massage, but there was no heat this time, only the mechanical movements of his hands working my muscles.

"You don't know if your parents are okay, either," he stated.

"No, I don't." I swallowed against the tightness that

had returned to my throat, trying to stick to my vow not to shed any more tears. It occurred to me then that Gabriel might be able to answer the question that had been plaguing me since the blackout had started. "Do you know how long it takes someone to die if they can't get access to a dialysis machine?" I rushed through the terrible words. I should have known the answer already, but I'd spent the past year pretending everything was fine. Avoiding knowledge of the thing I feared was part of that pretending.

"Is one of your parents on dialysis?" he asked. There was concern in his tone, and an unexpected compassion. The lump in my throat grew a little harder to swallow around.

"My mom has hep C. She doesn't go to dialysis every day, but if she can't get treatment...I just wonder if..." I couldn't bring myself to finish the thought.

I noticed his hands were soothing more than massaging now. I couldn't tell if he was aware of the change or simply lost in thought, but I took comfort from it nonetheless.

"Well, even people who need dialysis every day and can barely function without it have been known to live for months or even up to a year without treatment. I don't have her chart so I can't make a diagnosis, but I think your mom will be okay. Most hospitals have generators, so she may even still be getting treatments. You never know."

Relief flooded through me, and my throat tightened instead of loosening. There was a chance that she could survive this particular aspect of the blackout, and I was going to cling to it. It was a moment before I was able to speak again. "They're out in California. I don't know if they're even affected by whatever's going on here, but it's good to have one less thing to worry about."

"Man, I feel like an ass. Here I am complaining, and you have all that on your shoulders," he said.

"My parents' situation doesn't make your problems less important," I said. I tried to keep the misplaced annoyance out of my voice. I didn't deserve pity, and I didn't want it. He wouldn't give it to me so freely if he knew what a coward I'd been and the pain I'd caused my folks.

"I know," he said. "But at least I have my brother and sister with me." There was silence, and then he added, "And you."

"I thought I was a pain in your ass."

"You are," he said, "but that doesn't mean I can't appreciate having you around. You make John and Maggie happy for some reason."

Oh. I was annoyed at myself again for the pang of disappointment I felt, but grudging acceptance was better than the veiled threats from earlier, so I'd take it.

He gave my shoulders a final squeeze, and abruptly tugged my shirt back over my head to signal the massage was over.

"Wow, it doesn't feel like elves are shooting flaming arrows into my back anymore," I said as I stood up, bouncing my shoulders to show the improvement. I could move them without wincing in pain, which was pretty sweet. "Nice work, Doc Seong."

He gave the nonchalant shrug of a man who'd heard praise for his skills often before his gaze moved to my face. "That bruise on your jaw is pretty nasty. Let me check it out, too, while we're here. It looked fine in the clearing yesterday, but I was distracted, what with my brother bleeding out and all."

He was aiming for dark comedy, but his eyes dulled and shuttered after he spoke. Some emotions couldn't be hidden behind jokes. He was hard to figure out, this man who could be a hard-ass one minute and moved by his feelings for his family the next. I was disturbed by the fact that I *wanted* to figure him out. After our initial encounters, I'd figured we'd just live in détente until the crisis passed and I made my way home. One good massage later, and I was trying to get my Dr. Phil on with him. Not cool.

He stepped in front of me and cupped my chin in his hand, gingerly poking at my jaw. His face was close to mine, how it had been in the clearing. I remembered the way his gaze had lingered on me then. Now, he was all business, his gaze focused. His lips were moist and slightly parted, the scent of mint showing he'd had the decency to try to cover his kimchi breath before invading my personal space.

He grasped my jaw and gently pulled, forcing my mouth open. Although it wasn't the technique I was used to, I couldn't help but observe this was the perfect position for him to kiss me deep and hard. I closed my eyes so he couldn't read the lusty thoughts that now plagued me in his presence, but that made it all the easier to imagine him gripping my face as his mouth slanted over mine. I wished I'd had the foresight to get rid of my kimchi breath too.

"Does it hurt to open your mouth wide?" he asked, releasing his hold.

I don't know, why don't we do a little experiment? Unzip your pants. I kept that horrible pickup line to myself.

"Yeah, but I guess that's normal, considering how hard he hit me. I still can't believe he punched me. Twice," I said, trying to fix on something, anything, that wasn't the weird sensation Gabriel was evoking in me. Anger at Blue Hat would serve that purpose. "Asshole."

"Why did you fight them instead of just giving up your stuff?" Gabriel asked. "They were both at least double your size."

"Because they tried to kill my best friend." Bile rose in my throat when I remembered the way John had flailed as Blue Hat pulled off his pack. "I mean, I told them to just take our stuff and go, but they said no. The guy who hit me said John and I were considered provisions too. They were going to take us and do God knows what to us."

I shuddered as I remembered the sharky smile Blue Hat had given me. I knew what they would have done—to me, at least. I had teetered on the very edge of becoming a statistic, and no one would have ever known. But Gabriel had prevented that.

"So they were going to take you and John some-where?" Gabriel asked. I could tell by the way he cocked his head to the side that something was up. He glanced at the picture of his parents and then back at me. I was already shaking my head, my thoughts aligning with his.

"No. If they had your parents, they wouldn't have been after me and John."

"You can't know that," he said. "And your jaw is fine."

I grabbed Gabriel's wrist as he started to twist away from me, releasing it when I had his attention. There was so much emotion in his golden gaze: anger and hope, bound in frustration. I wished I'd kept my stupid mouth shut.

"Listen, I talked to those guys. I interacted with them. They were gross and smelly and hungry as hell," I said. "If they had intercepted your parents with a van full of supplies, they would have been a bit better off, don't you think?"

Gabriel made a dismissive noise. "I need to check—they could have gotten my parents on their way back, after they'd already dropped the stuff off with Darlene. I should run their pockets to see if I find any clues," he said, staring blankly across the room now as if he was already planning what he'd need for his trip back into the woods.

"No, what you should do is stay here and look after the family members you can account for instead of possi-bly getting yourself killed," I said and, with that, our brief truce was over. His eyes darkened to a heated bronze as he glared at me. I wanted to recoil, but never flinching was a point of pride. I met his gaze, no small part of me wishing the circumstances behind this tense staring match were entirely different.

"Look, you might know John, but you don't know me. You can save your opinions on the matter because they mean nothing to me," he said, his voice scathing. "If my parents are out there suffering and I don't try to help them, what kind of son am I? Would you leave your own parents to chance just because it wasn't easy?"

His words shocked me into silence. I pictured my mom connected to her dialysis machine but still smiling as we video-chatted. I remembered my last words to her, delivered over the phone because I'd been too much of a coward to see her reaction. *I'm sorry, I'm busy, I'll come in February instead.* I'd told myself it would be too hard to see her sick and defenseless, the woman who'd always been larger than life for me, but now I might never see her or my dad again. Thinking of how I'd treated them made me feel as if I was caught in the riptide of a crushing wave of regret, especially in the face of Gabriel's willingness to do anything for his parents, even revisiting that grisly scene. Pain and anger and helplessness coiled up inside me, twisting in my guts, and I lashed out at the closest target.

"You think you know better than everyone, but while you've been tucked away safely in the middle of nowhere, I've walked over a hundred miles. Let me tell you—things are fucked up out there, okay? No one knows what's going on, and people are doing crazy things. To flounce out of here on some knight-in-shining-armor quest to save your parents is stupid."

"It wasn't so stupid when I saved you and John yesterday, was it?" he countered.

"What you did was amazing, but it was a lucky accident," I said. "You weren't out in the woods pretending to be Rambo." I thought of how I'd first seen him, prowling through the trees with a rifle… "Wait. Is that what you were doing yesterday? Were you searching for your parents even though Maggie was alone?"

"That's none of your business," he growled, letting me know that I was right on the money.

"Actually, it is my business. What about the whole 'I would do anything to protect my family' line you gave me earlier?" I didn't understand how I could be so angry at him, this guy I hardly knew, but there was no denying it. My face was hot, my breath was coming fast. "Going out and getting yourself killed is not going to help John and Maggie. You need to think this through. Your parents are already gone, and if you don't come back, I'll be the one left to deal with the fallout."

"Well, you're always welcome to leave if you don't feel like dealing with it," he sneered.

"That's not my point and you know it." I was ready to burst with frustration. I didn't understand why we were arguing when, in the end, we both wanted what was best for John and Maggie.

"Right now, I don't care what your point is. I only care that, no matter how small the possibility, there may be something out there that leads to my parents," he said and stormed out of the room.

"Fine!" I yelled after him, my hands clenched into fists and, I'm fairly certain, steam coming out of my ears. I flopped down on the chair he'd abandoned and stared up at the picture of his parents. Given what I knew now, the guilt that threatened to overtake me at every thought of my parents, would I be able to stay put, knowing there was even the slightest chance I might be able to reach them? Probably not, but I also didn't have siblings to take into account.

He was right though. It wasn't my business what he did, even if some idiotic part of me seemed to care if he got hurt. Since when was I concerned about the actions of random doctors with attitude problems?

Stockholm syndrome, I thought bitterly.

I'd been stewing in my own juices for a little while when Maggie walked into the room, holding an acoustic guitar by its neck.

"Everything okay?" she asked with practiced light-heartedness as she sat on the arm of the sofa and began to strum. "We heard you and Gabriel arguing. Again."

"Gabriel and I appear to have many differences in opinion," I said diplomatically. It wasn't my place to tell her the cause of the argument.

"John has nicknamed you two Mr. and Mrs. Contentious," she said. "Like those children's books."

I rolled my eyes. "Where is John?"

"He's searching for something in his room," she said,

and then looked at me for a long moment. Right as her stare was bordering on creepy, she spoke. "It's good to finally meet someone who can get under Gabriel's skin. I love him, but he's way older than me and he's been so busy with med school that most of the time he just feels like another parent. But less fun than a parent, because he thinks he has to be serious with me all the time."

"Have you told him that?" He could be pretty annoying, but I'd seen the care and concern in his eyes when it came to his family.

"No," she said sullenly, retreating behind her thick fringe. "He thinks I'm just a kid and that he has to do everything for me, and set the right example and all that boring stuff. He won't even trust me to do things like get firewood and make dinner. And he doesn't tell me anything."

"He's a control freak, but he's not as bad as all that," I said, tugging at her hair. "Just like you're not used to him, he's not used to being around you. Maybe he thinks he's supposed to do everything for you. And he might not tell you anything because he thinks he can keep you safe that way."

"Maybe," she said in a distinctly unconvinced tone. She pushed the hair out of her face though. "But that doesn't mean it's not annoying. Anyway, I was going to ask if you could listen to me practice a little. Before all this stuff happened, I was trying to learn a song for…someone special. For a guy."

She looked at me expectantly. I'd spent so long trying to survive, and trying not to think about the outcome of this situation—whatever *this* was—that I hadn't given much thought to the opposite sex, except for the fear of strange men that had lingered at the back of my mind the whole trek up here.

The little ones are always feisty. My assailant's words resonated in my head. I shuddered, but then the memory of Gabriel's cool fingertips and how they'd eased my pain just a little emerged, pushing the terrifying thoughts away. I guess it wasn't entirely true that I hadn't thought of guys lately.

I realized Maggie was looking at me expectantly. "Sure. Go ahead and play it."

She started a clumsy chord progression that was hard for me to decipher at first, but then it clicked.

"One Direction?" I ventured.

"Yeah. Don't tell me you hate them, too," she cried out in dismay.

"Well, I wouldn't use the word *hate*." I'd first heard the boy band's music during my weekly spin class. Their songs were kind of infectious, but I wasn't going to admit that to anyone. My digital music files were inaccessible for the time being, so there was no physical evidence of my secret shame. "I know the song, but after this I'm teaching you some Velvet Underground."

"What is Velvet Underground?" she asked.

I tried to hide my dismay and simply said, "In the land of 1D, Velvet Underground is king. Let's work on this for now."

"Okay."

She ran through the song again, and I watched, adjusting her finger positioning and correcting her chords when necessary. I actually didn't have to do too much; her clumsiness on the first go through had been nerves.

"That was pretty good. You lied when you said you couldn't play."

"Whatever," she said, but her cheeks were rosy and a smile danced at the corners of her mouth. I was glad at least one of the new Seongs in my life seemed to like me. It was a nice change of pace.

"So who's the dude you were learning this song for?" I asked. I wasn't usually interested in teen intrigue, but Maggie had been stuck with Gabriel for days. She was probably starved for someone to talk girly stuff with and I wanted to indulge her, even if it wasn't my forte. Maybe I was actually the one who was starved for company.

"A friend," she said, her voice forlorn. She put down her guitar, carefully leaning it against the wall.

"This guy must be pretty special if you're learning a song for him. Not that it's any of my business." I picked at a cuticle to show my disinterest. After I managed to detangle my hair, I'd definitely need to give my woebegone nails some love too. I wasn't high-maintenance, but an apocalypse would wreak havoc on even the most minimalist of beauty routines.

Maggie pushed her long bangs out of her face and behind the shell of her ear, glancing around the room to make sure we were alone. "Don't tell my brothers, but I have a boyfriend," she said. Her eyes were wide with wonder, and there was a hint of pride in her tone.

"What's his name?" I asked, matching my low tones to hers.

"Devon," she sighed. "He lives in Florida."

"How—"

She cut me off before I could finish. "I met him online, on a guitar forum. He helped me understand basic music stuff—count, the different kind of notes, how to read music—things like that. I asked if he could help me figure out how to play a song, and he wrote the tab out for me by hand and mailed it to me. Like, snail mail!"

She gave a goofy laugh of surprise as she described the letter, the most romantic thing that had ever happened in her young life. I had to agree that it was pretty sweet. I gave her a sage nod of approval, and she continued excitedly.

"We started to video chat every night. We would practice guitar and just talk about life and what we wanted to do after high school...but now I don't even know if he's okay. He could be dead. Everyone could be, except for a handful of us." Maggie's eyes still shone, but not with excitement anymore. Her mouth twisted in an unsuccessful attempt to hide how her bottom lip trembled. "The not knowing is, like…I don't know. Like an annoying mosquito buzzing in my ear, driving me crazy, and there's nothing I can do to stop it."

I knew exactly what she meant, though I didn't feel like talking about it. Thoughts of my parents always hovered just on the edge of my consciousness, waiting for the smallest thing to remind me of them and prick my aching heart.

"What you're describing is totally normal, but we just have to be happy for the little things and try to stay positive," I said, hoping I sounded peppy and convincing, like the woman in the workout videos I'd watched on YouTube. "You have your brothers, you have food, you have warmth. Others were way less prepared for what happened. We can only hope that the people we care about are safe and that somehow they know we're safe too."

"You're right," she said. She twirled the ends of her long hair around her index finger. "I just miss him so much. It's like there's a constant pressure on my chest, and the more I think of how far away he is, the harder it pushes down on me. Have you ever felt that way?"

Another prick of the heart. I nodded.

"You know what? Let's try something," I said. "I saw this on one of those stupid daytime talk shows, and it's probably total BS, but it can't hurt to try. I want you to close your eyes and think 'I'm okay, and you're okay too.' Visualize Devon and your parents while you repeat that, and imagine them doing something like what we're doing now, or whatever would make them happy. Supposedly, if you put positive thoughts out into the universe, they can help shape the future. Or something. I don't know, just close your eyes."

"This is ridiculous, Arden," she huffed. Then her lids fluttered shut and she asked softly, "Do you really believe it'll work?"

"Let's hope so," I said and closed my eyes too. I imagined my parents sitting in their dining room at home, eating a salad fresh from the garden topped with my dad's prize-winning rutabaga. There was a knock at the front door— their neighbor, Mr. Klein, popping in to see if they needed anything. Lots of people checked in on them, so they never wanted for anything. My dad would offer Mr. Klein some of the good aged rum, and my mom would gently chide them both and then remind Dad to pour her a taste too. "We're doing fine. We just hope Arden is safe," she would say to Mr. Klein in that strong, smoky voice of hers, how she sounded when she was healthy and rested.

I am okay, Mom. I'm okay, and you guys are too.

"You know, I actually feel a bit better now...Arden?"

I opened my eyes to find Maggie peering at me with wide eyes. I wiped away the hot tears that had spilled down my cheeks without my knowledge. "Sorry, I got a little too into that exercise." I shrugged, trying to lighten the mood. "Awkwaaard."

Maggie handed me a tissue and was kind enough to look away as I blew my nose. "I want things to go back to normal," she said with a sigh.

"We'll try to be as normal as we can, I guess." Normal didn't make the pain and fear for those you cared about go away. Normal didn't take away your regrets. I'd spare her those harsh truths though; I suspected Maggie knew I was spouting nonsense, but a kid needed something to believe in. I did too.

She nodded, and then gave me a mischievous smile. "So is it 'normal' for a grown man and woman to fight like honey badgers but look at each other like they're going to start sucking face any second?"

"Maggie!" I swatted at her.

"What?" she asked, throwing up an elbow in defense. "I'm just a girl trying to figure things out with the help of my elders. I don't think trying to scratch each other's eyes out is a healthy way of showing affection."

"You have much to learn, kid," I muttered.

John walked in then, settling on the sofa with a blanket and a battered copy of *Watership Down*. He lifted his head and flared his nostrils in an exaggerated sniff. "Why does it smell like Tiger Balm in here?" he asked.

I flushed immediately under his knowing gaze. "Gabriel thought it would help with my back."

His eyes narrowed appraisingly, but he opened the book and flipped to the first page with feigned disinterest in what I'd said. Maggie practiced strumming chords. I could see a smirk on the section of face visible beneath her swinging bangs.

John licked his index finger and flipped a page before asking, "So, were you guys arguing over who rubbed down whom first?"

"No, it was...something else," I said guiltily. I didn't want to hide anything from them, especially from John. Getting in the middle of Seong family problems didn't seem like a good idea. If Gabriel was dead set on going out searching, he could be the one to explain it to them.

"You guys have only talked to each other for, oh, I'd say an hour total, when you take things like passing out, bathing and daydreaming about our impending doom into consideration, but you've managed to argue for fifty-nine of those sixty minutes. Interesting, huh?"

"You forgot that they worked a massage in there, too," Maggie said before striking a perfect power chord.

"It was a medical massage, performed by a licensed doctor," I said. "Nice chord, by the way. That was really clean."

"Nice attempt to change the subject. Not very clean, though," John said, placing his book in his lap and leaning forward to squint at me. "Oh. Of course! I can't believe I didn't think of this! Gabriel is all controlling and anal and annoying. Of course he'd fall for an angry, independent, free-spirited woman like you." He shook his head in disgust and picked up the book again. "You guys are *so* cliché."

"No one is falling for anyone," I said. "You guys are just going through reality TV withdrawal." Despite my protestations, a little shiver of pleasure shook me as I remembered Gabriel's strong hands and how expertly they'd discovered and eased the painful knots in my back. I wondered if he'd be as intuitive when it came to touching me in other places too.

"Mom would've seen it coming from a mile away," Maggie said, quietly strumming a D minor chord. "She was always trying to play matchmaker."

"Wasn't she?" John chimed in from behind the pages of his book. "The first thing she said when I came out was 'Oh, Mrs. Kim's nephew is gay too! He's a nice boy. I'll call her and arrange a coffee date, Jang-Wan.'"

We all laughed. I looked at the picture above the mantle again, at the vibrancy and love in his parents' eyes. Of course Gabriel wanted to go find them.

"My mom stopped setting me up after I told the pastor's son I was into Satan worship and blood sacrifice," I said.

Maggie snorted out a laugh, and John tilted his head in my direction, his bandage making him look like a deranged tennis player.

"So you really were always this charming," he said.

"I came straight out of the womb kicking ass and tak-ing names," I said, throwing a few fake jabs toward Maggie.

"Gross," she exclaimed as she jumped off the arm of the couch. "I'm gonna go practice in my room before you start talking about swinging the placenta around your head by the umbilical cord."

"Get out," John ordered. "Get out before Arden cor-rupts you any further."

"A girl after my own heart," I said after she left. "I really do like her. Kind of makes me wish I had some siblings."

"You were more than enough for your parents to han-dle, I'm sure," John said. His eyes trailed Maggie as she walked up the stairs. "And you've got me, so you don't need any siblings. Besides, it would just mean more people for you to worry about now."

I sighed and walked over to the bookcase to find something to read. Cormac McCarthy's *The Road* caught my eye, but I remembered seeing the trailer for the movie adaptation and immediately vetoed it. Next to it was an old book with a peeling spine that seemed as if it might hold my attention. I grabbed it and settled back onto the sofa.

"God, Fiver!" John cried out a long while later. "Ugh, I always forget how emotional this book makes me. What're you reading?"

I'd been so absorbed in my book that I hadn't noticed the time fly by. Even though we were in a room with boarded-up windows, I could sense it was starting to get dark out. Perhaps my time spent outdoors had rebooted my circadian rhythm.

"*Love in the Western World*," I answered. "It's old, but pretty interesting stuff."

"Fascinating choice," he said, raising a brow at me. "That's Gabriel's book from college. Maybe you could ask him to share some insight about it with you?"

I threw John a look, but realized he hadn't been teasing. I wondered where Gabriel had been for the past few hours. Would he have left without saying anything? Was he out there in the dark woods? "Valentine's Day was last week, you know. I'm just trying to get into the holiday spirit."

"Fuck, was it?" John asked. "Well, I guess the only thing different about this year is that I actually have a good excuse for not having a Valentine. 'Oh, all the good men got Raptured away/abducted by aliens/are huddled in bunkers wondering whether the world is ending. You know how it is.'"

"Well, this book hasn't been too uplifting. Basically, love is a myth and has been perverted by Western culture as a substitute for true self-awareness, which can only be reached in death."

John splayed open his book and fanned himself with the pages. "Sounds like some sexy stuff, Arden," he said. "Please stop, I don't think my loins will be able to stand much more."

I stood and stretched languorously before remembering that I should have been howling in pain from the motion. Gabriel really did have magic fingers. "Okay, I'll spare you a case of burst loins," I said, walking toward the door. "That would be an awkward medical problem, since your brother is the only doctor we have now."

He rolled his eyes. "My loins will remain intact for the foreseeable future, I imagine," he said, a frown marring his face. I wondered if his head was hurting him, or his heart. But then the moment passed and he was dry, witty John again. "You know, you should probably skip the love-and-death stuff when it comes to Gabe. Just stick to your tried-and-true method of beating men into submission."

I frowned at him, but not because of his critique of my dating style. "I don't think beating your brother into submission would be a good idea," I said. I couldn't tell if he was joking or not, but given my reaction to Gabriel, I didn't find it humorous.

"Why not? I always said when the apocalypse came I'd want to be coming, too," he said. He gave me an apologetic smirk for his bad joke before continuing. "I'm not saying you have to marry him, but if you have certain urges you shouldn't deny them on my account. There really isn't a better time to act on inappropriate sexual impulses, if you ask me."

"Not that there are any impulses to act on," I hedged, "but are you sure you wouldn't mind?"

"I'm actually kind of jealous," he admitted. "It would be nice to have someone to lean on right now."

What did he mean? Was he feeling neglected? Had I let him down, after all he'd done for me by bringing me with him? "I'm here for you to lean on."

"Let me rephrase that. It would be nice to have someone to have crazy, sweaty, end-of-days sex with right now," he said, and then pretended to gag. "Ew, I can't believe I'm talking about this in the context of my brother. Please go before you cause my psyche irreparable damage."

I went up to the room I shared with John. As I lay in the single bed, I thought of what John had said about having someone to lean on.

That's probably the reason I find Gabriel attractive. He's the only available man around in a stressful situation, and I'm just trying to find some comfort. I'd be better off sticking with my hand.

I'd made it a rule never to be with a man because I needed him. I'd been raised to stand on my own two feet. I didn't need a guy to take care of me, especially one who displayed such an obvious need to be in control all the time.

Still, as I drifted to sleep, I thought of how pleasant Gabriel had been when he'd examined me, and how he'd been playful and gentle while he'd massaged the balm into my weary body.

Maybe it wasn't just desperation after all.

7

I woke with a start in the middle of the night. My heart thudded in my chest and my mouth was wide open, curved around the silent scream that had driven me from my nightmare.

In the dream, Blue Hat held me down like he had in real life, but this time blood and gore dripped from his wound, hot splashes on my face and in my mouth as I screamed and screamed. I lay paralyzed with fear immediately after I woke up and for a horrible, confusing moment I was positive he was in the room with me, that the safe haven of the cabin had been breached.

I tried to get my panicked breathing under control, my gaze darting around the room as if Blue Hat had crossed over from my nightmares into the realm of the living. There was no one else in the room but John, who snored and clutched one of his pillows to his chest. That didn't stop the panic from cresting again.

I instinctively reached for my Louisville Slugger—I usually slept with it propped beside my bed—but grabbed a handful of darkness instead. It was then that I realized I had left it behind in the clearing after the attack. The bat had been a gift from my dad when I'd moved to New York. He'd joked that I might need to bust a few skulls in his stead, but it had served as my talisman to keep the boogeymen away, and I desperately needed that kind of magic just then. The dream had been so real...

He's dead. He can't hurt you, I repeated to myself, the words eventually helping to calm me. I lay staring at the ceiling for a long time, but I couldn't get back to sleep knowing what horrible possibilities awaited me in my dreams. Instead, a barrage of unwanted thoughts assailed me.

What if someone else attacks us? What if we never find out what happened and this is where I'll be stuck for the rest of my life? What if I never see my parents again? Could a nuclear bomb have gone off without me knowing? What if there's something even more terrible than anything we can imagine awaiting us?

When I got sick of driving myself crazy, I threw the covers off and hopped out of the bed. I grabbed the small battery-powered lantern from my nightstand and tiptoed across the room, waiting until I reached the hallway to turn on the light.

Fear of being alone in an unfamiliar house in the

dead of night nagged at me as I crept down the stairs, but I chided myself for being ridiculous. I had slept on roadsides and in the middle of the woods. I was safe now. I was sheltered and warm, and the bad guys couldn't reach me inside this place. At least I hoped they couldn't.

I had gotten all the way to the kitchen when I heard the floorboard creak behind me.

"Guess I'm not the only one who can't sleep." Gabriel spoke in a low voice that was gritty with fatigue.

I whirled, catching him in the dim beam of my lantern. The light played across his face, highlighting his sharp cheekbones and the dark recesses beneath his eyes. The effect should have been ghoulish, but instead it gave me insight into why so many of my friends were into movies about sexy vampires.

"Sorry, I didn't mean to scare you," he said. There was a certain caution, a distance, in his tone that reminded me that his last words to me had been spoken in anger. But right now I didn't feel like fighting with him or thinking about my nightmares. I just wanted to drink something warm that would help lull me to sleep.

"You didn't scare me," I said. He walked around me and lit one of the candles on the kitchen table, so I turned off my lantern. "I was just surprised to see anyone else up and about."

"I've always been a night owl, and I became an even bigger one once I started my shifts at the hospital," he said with a shrug.

"I thought doctors were able to fall asleep anytime, anywhere." I placed the lantern down and looked around for a teakettle. "That's what happens on the TV shows."

"Too much television will rot your brain, Arden," he chided, moving past me and grabbing the kettle from a high shelf over the stove. "And I guess I'm not like most doctors."

"How did you know I was looking for the teakettle?" I asked, watching as he poured water from a bucket into the kettle and then placed it onto the low flame of a camping stove. "And what's so different about you?"

Since he was in control of the beverage situation, I curled up in one of the wide-bottomed kitchen chairs and pulled the long sweater over my knees. It was hard not to stare at the way his broad shoulders moved beneath his long-sleeved shirt, how his waist narrowed and his sweatpants hung from his slim hips.

"I'm not some kind of special snowflake. It's just really hard for me to let things go," he said.

"Oh, really? You could have fooled me," I said with a teasing grin.

He laughed and ruffled a hand through his hair. "Yeah, I guess I walked into that. It's hard to fall asleep on any available flat surface when I can't get my thoughts to slow down. It was bad enough when I was in school, but when I started my residency I wasn't always able to shake the things I'd seen during a shift. These days…a good night's sleep is pretty much impossible." He grabbed a couple of mugs from a cabinet and placed one in front of me, and then grabbed a box of sleep-aid tea and shook it in my direction. "And I knew you were looking for tea because I was too. I don't really take you for a warm-glass-of-milk kind of woman."

"You have read me correctly." I crossed my arms over my knees, tilting my head to observe him. It was hard to imagine Gabriel sitting up at night fretting, like I did. He seemed so competent and in control. It was reassuring to know that even he was tortured by neuroses, like us mere mortals.

"Why'd you become a doctor?" I asked. I didn't want to be nosy, but it was the kind of thing you should know about a person you were trapped with for the foreseeable future.

"Because I have a God complex," he responded with a stony expression, and then burst out laughing at my shocked reaction. "I don't know. It just seemed like the thing to do. I'd get to help people, and one day I'd make enough money to provide for my parents so they wouldn't have to work so hard all the time. Plus, people would have to call me Doctor."

"That's the only reason you did it, isn't it?" I teased. Why was it so easy for us to talk now? Maybe this was his doppelgänger, who was only allowed up from the cellar at night. Tomorrow, the real Gabriel would have no idea what I was talking about if I mentioned this conversation.

"That and the nurses," he replied with a wink. I wrinkled my nose in disdain, and he raised his hands. "Kidding.

Just kidding. Ninety percent of the nurses would rather kick me than kiss me."

"Sounds reasonable to me," I said. My cheeks warmed when he gave me a narrow look, as if trying to decide whether I'd be categorized as a ninety-percenter or with the remaining ten. I quickly changed the subject. "I know we talked about it earlier, but you really don't have any idea what's going on?"

"No. I know stuff was going down with the Russians, but this seems way too crazy for a first strike, right? If this was war, I think we'd know it." He glanced at the teakettle, and then reached out to turn up the flame on the camp stove. "I wish I could say that people started staggering into the hospital with a craving for brains, or that there was some pandemic, but things were fine before I left. Hell, things didn't even get that bad until my parents didn't come back. That's when I realized how completely screwed we were."

"Way to be optimistic," I said.

He cut his glance at me and then saw the tight smile on my face and returned it.

"It was starting to get really bad in Rochester," I said abruptly. I had intended to leave it at that, but the words continued to flow of their own volition. "We stayed indoors once we realized that law and order had become a self-serve situation, but we could still hear stuff that was really scary. The night we decided to leave, we heard a woman scream for help. I've never heard anyone yell like that before." I stopped and took a deep breath to quell my nerves. I didn't know why, but it seemed important that someone else know what had happened. "The screaming stopped, but then we heard a group of men whooping and laughing and making lewd comments—and then nothing."

"Christ, Arden." He didn't say anything more, but his deep voice conveyed concern and disgust in those two words. The kettle began to sound then, and Gabriel removed it from the flame before the soft whistling could become a full-on shriek.

"I tell myself that she got away, but the way those men laughed... That was when we decided to go. John said we had to leave before things got any worse, and I couldn't argue with that. We packed up and left the next morning."

I didn't mention how the woman's voice had been familiar, even distorted by distress. Had it really been Kerry, the woman who lived in the next condo over with her two cats, making that guttural cry for help? She'd once given me a homemade cupcake, still warm from the oven, when she'd seen me reading in the laundry room. Horrible things shouldn't happen to people who gave baked goods to near strangers, but I'd seen one of her calicoes scratching at her front door when John and I had set out. It had still been there, meowing anxiously, when we'd turned the corner and headed for the outskirts of town.

Gabriel poured our tea in silence and sat down across from me. I cradled the teacup in my hands as it steeped, the ceramic warm against my cold fingers. It had a floral scent, designed to calm frayed nerves. I inhaled deeply.

"That must have made the attack the other day even worse for you. You guys were so close, and what you were running from almost caught up to you anyway," he said. His head jerked toward me, the candlelight flickering in his gaze as it locked on mine. "He didn't...they didn't hurt you anywhere else, did they?"

I shook my head. A violent shudder passed through me at the thought of what had almost happened. I felt as if I had no right to wallow in fear over *almost;* what was a close call for me was a terrible reality for so many others. But the strangers who'd attacked us were haunting my thoughts as much as my parents and friends, and the farther I got from the event, the more frightening it became.

"I don't want to talk about this anymore," I said. I was aiming for cavalier, but my tea sloshing over the side of my cup blew my cover. I hated how my hands shook when I thought of what could have happened to John and me; it felt too much like Blue Hat still had physical control over my body, even if he'd never touch me again. I placed the tea down and clasped my hands between my thighs, hiding them until I was able to get the tremors under control. It wasn't as easy to control the sweat that pricked at my hairline and the brief certainty that I was going to puke.

"What did you do in Rochester, before this happened? What kind of job did you have? What kind of boss?" Gabriel asked, changing the subject to something that didn't distress me. Here, in the dim silence of the kitchen, Gabriel seemed able to read my reactions so easily. More than that, he seemed to be conscious of how what he said and did affected me. I chalked it up to his profession—maybe he'd decided to grease up that rusty bedside manner he'd mentioned.

"I'm a bookkeeper," I answered. "My boss is pretty freaking awesome, since I work for myself, although several other people think otherwise. I manage the accounts for a few restaurants and small businesses, make sure their books are in order and give them tips on how to better manage their money. Or I did before...this."

"Really?" he asked, unable to keep the shock from his voice.

And here I'd thought he was so intuitive. "What do you mean, 'really'?" I asked, not bothering to veil the annoyance in my voice. I'd met plenty of men who doubted my ability to do my job because I was a woman or because I was black or both; I didn't need it from Gabriel.

"What are you getting mad about? I mean, come on. That sounds like such a boring job," he said, taking a sip of his tea, and then wincing because it hadn't cooled down yet.

"That's what you get for making fun of my profession," I said, slightly mollified by both his explanation and the way he ran his tongue over the bow of his lip to soothe the burn. I had never admired someone's tongue before, but I was struck by his. It seemed rather...long. And flexible. I shifted in my seat, wondering if he was as good with his tongue as he was with his hands. Given what I knew of him, there was no reason to think his skills would be lacking.

"I imagined you being, I don't know, pre-law or something more fitting of your personality." His voice pulled me away from my reverie, although judging from his smirk, he had caught me staring at his mouth. I wasn't shy by any means, but I flushed and looked away as he continued. "Maybe things were different before, but the Arden I know wouldn't be fulfilled by a job like that."

"Do you know another Arden? Because I'm pretty sure you don't know me at all," I said testily.

"Fair enough," he said, his eyes still on me. He smiled a bit and lowered his head, and I realized I had proven his point.

I traced my finger around the tea-warmed rim of my mug. I had never *felt* like a bookkeeper, but that was the job I'd fallen into right after college. I'd started doing the books for the pub I waitressed at, and then the place across the street, and it paid the bills. It was dependable, and I didn't even have to try very hard most of the time. What did Gabriel think he knew about me that he could imagine me as a lawyer instead?

"Hey, I'm not trying to dis your job. It's just that you're, too…too, Arden to be a bookkeeper." He raised his cup to his lips and blew across the surface before taking a sip.

I rolled my eyes, but mostly to hide the fact that I was confused by his words. He'd said "too Arden" like it was a good thing, something I'd never considered before. "Anyway, that's what I did. I play guitar and sing at pubs in town sometimes, which is fun, but I wasn't going to be the next Joni Mitchell. I wasn't passionate about anything," I said with a sigh. "It's kind of pathetic actually. Once all this craziness started to sink in, I was forced to realize that if the world were ending, I'd have accomplished nothing that I really cared about."

I finally took a sip of my tea, surprised by my confession. I felt exposed and wished the floral-scented steam rising from my mug could hide me from Gabriel's inquisitive gaze. I was quickly coming to understand that apocalyptic situations had a way of lowering one's inhibitions.

"I get you," he said. "After a few days of being stuck here, not knowing what's going on, I started to have some thoughts that weren't helpful, to say the least. I think I went a little crazy, boarding up the house and going out looking for trouble. I certainly found it."

Silence stretched taut between us.

"Are you going out to search the bodies?" I finally asked. "Please don't go alone."

"I thought we were supposed to be doing the getting-to-know-you thing," he said, dodging my question.

"Were we now?" I asked. "I thought we were doing the trick-Gabriel-into-making-me-tea thing."

He laughed, and the sound hit me low and vibrated through my body. All my inappropriate thoughts from throughout the night coalesced into a call to action. Wondering how his tongue felt wasn't enough, I had to *know*. How could a simple sound wave start the chain reaction of want so easily? Maybe it was because it was such an easy, comfortable laugh, the kind you shared before climbing into bed next to someone or spending a quiet night on the couch. Unfortunately, Gabriel wasn't the kind of person I should be doing either of those things with. I stayed in my seat.

"So, are you going to go back to hating me anytime soon?" I asked. "This is nice, but I like to be prepared for disappointment." John often had to point out when I was being abrupt or performing what he liked to call the self-sabotage shuffle, but even I could tell I'd just gone and ruined a perfectly nice moment.

"I'm not going to keep apologizing," Gabriel said bluntly, his smile fading. "Before, you were a mouthy stranger whose actions put my brother in danger, and possibly my sister too. I know you're an only child, but you have to be able to understand that."

I may not have had siblings, but I knew what it was to fear for your family. Beyond that, I knew what it was to let them down. I thought of my dad's salt-and-pepper mustache drooping as he frowned. My mom's sallow skin beneath her silver curls. Tears heated my eyes, and I grimaced, trying to keep them at bay.

"I understand," I said. "You were right. I'm impulsive and I don't think about the outcome of my actions until it's too late."

I stared into my teacup, but I still saw his hand as it reached across the table. I focused on the way it was golden in the candlelight instead of how good it felt when he laid it on my arm.

"No, I wasn't right. It's good that you're here," he said.

"Why?" I asked suspiciously.

His gaze met mine and he laughed quietly, standing and gathering his mug. "I'll add 'can't take a compliment' to your patient profile."

At that, he bid me good-night and walked off into the darkness. I could still feel his touch on my arm when I finally picked up my cup with steady hands and drained the tea down to the dregs. I couldn't tell if it was some potent mix of herbs and flowers or the conversation with Gabriel, but I felt slightly more at peace.

It's good that you're here. I wanted to believe those words, but the last people who'd depended on me had probably realized by now that they'd expected too much. I hoped for John's, Gabriel's and Maggie's sakes that I wouldn't screw up this time around.

8

The next morning I made a breakfast of instant oatmeal with raisins for everyone, but Gabriel had apparently already eaten and told John he was going for a walk. John was dispassionate as he delivered the news, and Maggie was slightly peeved that she wasn't allowed to go. Neither of them seemed to have guessed the true reason for his excursion.

I kept my face neutral even though my stomach flipped at the news. Had he really just left without telling anyone his plan? Why hadn't he asked for my help? I'd thought we'd made a connection over our teacups, but in the end he'd ignored my plea that he not go alone. Despite my anger, I hoped he would be okay. I didn't know if I should hope that his hunch was right—if it was, their parents were definitely in trouble.

I spent the next few hours nervous and fidgety, wondering if I should mention that Gabriel might be looking for their parents to John and Maggie. I didn't want to get their hopes up or have them go charging out of the house after him, so I kept my mouth shut. I felt as if I was making the right decision, but withholding information from my best friend—lying, essentially—felt awful. My resentment of Gabriel's actions grew as the day crawled forward and I slunk around the house, hiding from John's and Maggie's growing concern.

I threw myself into household chores, eager for a distraction. The place was already clean, so I decided to wash the clothes John and I had worn during our journey.

I didn't want to waste clean water from the cistern, so I hauled in snow from outside and melted it in pots on the stove to get water for the laundry. I hadn't carried any heavy loads since the massage, and I was pleased to find there was barely any pain in my back and shoulders as I worked.

Gathering the snow was the first time I'd gone outside since John and I had arrived. The day was freezing and amazingly bright in contrast to the dim interior of the house. The boarded-up windows would deter intruders, but they kept out light, as well.

The air was crisp and carried the scent of pine sap. The only sound was the wind shushing through the trees and the occasional fall of snow sliding from branches. The scenery was reminiscent of a Bob Ross watercolor. It should have felt freeing to be outside, but a bubble of fear welled up in me instead. Anyone could be hiding behind those happy little trees, waiting in ambush like Blue Hat and his partner had a few days before.

I hurried inside with the last pail of snow, ashamed at how relieved I felt when I locked the door and leaned back against it. I thought about Gabriel trudging through the woods alone and felt a sickening pang of fear for him. I'd have given anything for a quick text message or social media status update right then. *just searched some dead bodies and saved my parents, like a boss. brb.* There was no point in obsessing over his safety though. All I could do was hope for his return. I threw myself back into my chores with vigor.

"How quaint," John said when he popped into the bathroom as I leaned over the tub to rinse out our freshly washed clothing. "Making breakfast, doing laundry—you're a regular Betty Homemaker."

I flicked water at him, and he skittered back dramatically.

"I'm just trying to keep busy," I said, flashing a smile at his theatrics. "It's kind of relaxing to focus on putting things in order. And it would be nice to have some clean underwear. I refuse to wear Maggie's. That's just a bridge too far for me right now."

John watched me struggle to wring a pair of jeans dry. He came over and took one end of the pants and began twisting the fabric in the opposite direction. We worked silently, but from the set of John's mouth I could tell he wanted to say something.

Did he know where Gabriel had gone? Did he suspect I was keeping something from him? How was it that I now shared a secret with Gabriel instead of my best friend?

He finally spoke. "Arden, do you think things are ever going to be okay? It's been weeks."

I stared at the blue-tinged water dripping from the denim as we twisted it, tighter and tighter. This was the kind of question I'd sought to avoid with my cleaning spree, and I felt a surge of anger at him for asking me point-blank the thing that terrified me the most. What did it matter if things got better? What did any of it matter? But when I looked at that sweet face of his, at the way he twitched his nose because his hands were too occupied to scratch it, I realized that it did matter. If it didn't, what was this warmth that filled my heart when I looked at my best friend? What was this desire to comfort him when I didn't have the tiniest scrap of evidence we'd be okay? That feeling was something stronger than terror, and I could only hope it would see us through.

"I don't know, John," I answered truthfully. "I don't know if things are ever going to be the same, but I have to think they'll get better. I mean, humans were built to last. If the world blows up, that's one thing, but as long as there's land to stand on, people won't disappear without a fight."

He shook his head in exasperation. "But what if this is it for us?" He had stopped wringing and was staring at me. "What if I never get to play an online RPG again? Never post a snarky comment about the latest iOS upgrade? What if I never live tweet a bad movie, or humiliate a corporation by co-opting their hashtag? Worse than all that, what if all the work I put into curating my porn Tumblr was for naught? Do I really want to live in a world where all the online street cred I accrued over the years means nothing?"

I was tempted to laugh, not out of lack of empathy, but because the name of his microblog, *Fuzzy Wuzzy Banged A Bear*, got me every time. But the frown lines that creased his cheeks and the anxiety in his eyes put that brief temptation to rest.

"Well, if things never go back to normal, then we'd better get a washboard because this isn't going to cut it," I said. I stood and pulled the jeans from his hands and tried to shake out the wrinkles. "And there's always Dungeons & Dragons instead of online RPGs. You can be my dungeon master anytime."

He smirked, but it didn't reach his eyes. He went silent instead of snarking back, which scared me. He didn't even shoo me away when I shook a rain of water droplets in his direction. When I was feeling optimistic about our survival and John looked hopelessly adrift, there was a major problem.

"Is your head doing okay?" I asked.

"There's an ache that comes and goes, but it hurts a lot less."

I nodded, unsure if that was a good or bad symptom. "Do you have a headache right now?"

"No."

"Good. I won't feel bad asking you to show me how to make a fire so we can dry these clothes."

He nodded unenthusiastically but seemed to lighten up a little while teaching me his tried-and-true technique for starting a fire with just his hands, a stick and a board. "It's funny the Scouts are so anti-gay. They taught me everything I know about handling wood," he said as we watched the fire crackle to life.

After laying out our clothes, I carried a final pot of heated water up to the bathroom. Using a bit of conditioner and the razor Maggie had given me, I shaved my legs and underarms. I thoroughly conditioned my hair, and then plaited it into two simple braids so it wouldn't be too out of control when it was fully dried.

Doing chores, followed by the ritual acts of hygiene that I'd foregone for so long, gave me a sense of normalcy that seemed almost alien in its mundanity.

I examined myself in the mirror, glad to see the dark circles under my eyes had faded and I didn't look quite so haggard. The bruise still marred my cheek, but I was on my way to feeling human again.

Gabriel showed up as evening was settling over the house. It was hard to tell exact time, with the windows boarded up and no analog clocks in the vicinity, but something changed in the air that signaled the coming of night.

Maggie, John and I were milling about the kitchen, warming up the last of the stew that we'd eaten for lunch and dinner for the past few days.

"Where the hell have you been?" John asked flatly as soon as the back door swung open, letting in a frigid gust of air. He hadn't said anything since night fell, but I'd seen him giving the door sidelong glances.

Gabriel closed the door behind him and stomped the snow off his boots. His face was ruddy from the cold and his clothes were covered with mud. His gaze was dull and closed-off when he looked at John. "I was checking something out, like I told you I was going to," he said, heading into the hallway to hang his coat. He moved stiffly, and I wondered if it was from being outside in the cold all day or if he had injured himself.

"You didn't say you were going to be gone for so long," John pushed. Maggie had frozen on the other side of the room, tensing for whatever her two older brothers were about to get into.

"I didn't know I would be," Gabriel said, stepping into the kitchen and into the nightly dinner routine as if he'd been there all along. As if three people hadn't spent the day carefully avoiding mentioning how long he had been gone.

Maggie made a disgruntled noise. I turned to catch her mouth pull down into a frown, but then the anxiety John had kept corked exploded from him.

"I know you're an insensitive ass, but I was worried all fucking day, and so were Maggie and Arden. Mom and Dad are missing, Arden and I got attacked by freaks and you're fine with just traipsing off for hours without letting us know you're okay?"

Gabriel paused, his gaze flicked to me for a second, and then back to John. "I'm sorry," he said in a voice strained by fatigue. "I went back to where I found you guys to move the bodies somewhere less exposed. I needed a little time to myself after that. Is that okay with you?"

"Okay, and now I feel like an asshole," John said, crossing his arms over his chest. "But I can't help that I was worried about you, can I?"

"No, Jang-Wan, but you should trust that I wouldn't leave you guys alone without good reason," he said, his gaze moving in my direction again. Was he surprised that I hadn't ratted him out? Had he expected me to?

"You can't just keep doing things without letting us know!" Maggie shouted suddenly. "It's not fair. You don't tell me anything, and you don't care if I'm scared because I don't even know what's going on in our own house, let alone outside of it!"

There was so much anger and frustration in her voice that it was effective as a whip crack at shutting everyone up. I realized that she'd been cooped up with Gabriel for days and days after living only with her parents; it was understandable that she'd finally reached a breaking point.

Gabriel's eyebrows shot up in confusion. "Maggie, what do you mean? I do tell you things, and if I don't it's because I *don't* want you to be scared."

"I'm not a little kid," she said, but she delivered her announcement in such a petulant manner that I couldn't help but think otherwise. I wanted to say something to make this all stop; however, Maggie barely knew me and she needed to hear it from Gabriel.

He drew in a deep breath and ran a hand through his hair in frustration. "I know you're not a kid," he said. "I know you're smart and resourceful and that you want to help. But my job is to protect you. I was just trying to keep things as normal as possible for you. I'm sorry if I made you feel unneeded."

Maggie bobbed her head in a nod that showed her confusion; she still wanted to fight, but Gabriel had actually agreed with what she said. "Just, don't keep things from me anymore, okay?"

"I'll try not to," he said, but his eyes lingered meaningfully on mine, putting me on alert. "Can we just have a happy family dinner now?"

We were mostly silent throughout the meal. Maggie sulked behind her bangs, and everyone seemed lost in interior contemplation while they ate. I spent most of the meal wondering what Gabriel had seen and trying to suss out why I'd been so worried while he was gone. I'd just met him; hell, I didn't even like him most of the time, and he didn't seem to like me much either, right? But I'd felt a weight lift off my chest when he'd walked in the back door.

I ventured a glance across the table. He was rearranging the food on his plate with the incongruously fancy chopsticks we'd been using at meals. His golden gaze flashed to mine, and I was paralyzed, unable to look away from the tumult of emotions I saw at play. He looked away quickly, but something in his gaze had touched on that needy part of me that had been improbably awakened since I'd first met him in the midst of snow and gore.

"I'm going to go do some inventory in the cellar and see what our supplies are like," Gabriel said suddenly, his voice rough. He left in haste, his food half-eaten.

"This really sucks," John said, laying his chopsticks down on the table. "What am I supposed to say to him? 'So, thanks for killing and disposing of those freaks who tried to knock my brain out, brother, and sorry I was an anxious jerk who blew up at you for no reason'?"

"Um, I'm pretty sure I win the sibling spaz-out award, John," Maggie said as she scraped together the last of the rice grains in her bowl.

"I think he understands," I said. "He probably just needs to take a few minutes to decompress after what sounds like a shitty day."

I talked a good game, but the desire to go to Gabriel had been on me the moment he'd stood. I told myself I was just curious to hear what he'd found and ask what that pointed look had been about, but the undercurrent to that curiosity was the need to make sure he was okay. Not the jerky, control freak Gabriel, but the caring doctor who tended to our wounds after killing for us, the man who so desperately wanted his parents to be okay.

"I think you should go talk to him," John said with a glance in my direction.

"What? Why?" I stayed seated, although in my mind I was already halfway down the cellar stairs.

"Because he might need to talk. He's so used to being mother hen to me and Maggie that he'd just tell us he's okay so we don't feel bad," John said. "With you, there's at least a chance that he'll be willing to unload some of what's bothering him."

"Okay, I guess I'll go," I said in a put-upon tone as I headed toward the cellar door. "If you think that's best."

"Oh, please. Who does she think she's kidding?" John asked Maggie. I pretended I didn't hear.

The cellar was low-ceilinged and lined with shelves, which were themselves lined with jars. Stacks of grocery store inventory filled most of the floor space: palettes of pinto beans, boxes of beef stew. A single lightbulb cast a dim glow about the loamy smelling room. I'd expected it to be damp and cold, but it was dry and only slightly chilly.

I stepped around a stack of boxes and came upon Gabriel holding a jar of pickled vegetables up to the light. "Need help?"

He fumbled the jar, we both lunged and it ended up securely wrapped in two sets of hands. I relinquished my grip and stepped back, raising my palms in apology.

"Jesus, can you not creep up on me when I'm holding part of our limited food supply?" he snapped. He placed the jar back on the shelf and sketched a mark in a notebook that lay close by. His head almost brushed against the ceiling of the enclosed space, making him seem even taller and more imposing.

"Sorry. I'll save my creeping for more appropriate times," I said. Why had I wanted to come down here again? Every interaction between us thus far, minus one, had ended with Gabriel acting like a prick and me either yelling at him or getting my feelings hurt.

"Do you need something?" he asked, still curt.

I need you to stop acting like an uptight jerk, I thought, but then remembered what I'd actually wanted to say, which was much more civil. "I just wanted to apologize for yesterday. I should have done it when we spoke last night. You were right—it wasn't my place to tell you what to do when it comes to your family. It's just...I care about John. And even though I've just met you and Maggie, I care about you guys too. I do want to punch you sometimes, but I don't know what they'd do if anything happened to you."

He stopped examining jars to glance at me. He didn't speak for a long moment, probably waiting for some catch to my apology, but there was none. "No need for that," he said, his voice a little less harsh. "You were right. I knew you were right, but I still had to go and see anyway. It would have driven me crazy otherwise, knowing there was something, anything, I could do to find them."

"I shouldn't have been so confrontational about it," I said, ignoring the way my guts twisted as I thought of my own parents. "I wish I had the opportunity to do the same for my folks."

"I believe that. You seem to be just as stubborn as I am," he said. "That's why it's good you're here. I need someone who'll call me out on my shit, and you have no problem doing that."

Yesterday he'd said that John and Maggie needed me, but now he needed me for something, too, even if it was just to be a pain in his ass. To my dismay, I felt the heat of the blush as it suffused my cheeks. I was definitely getting soft—pre-blackout me would've already cussed him out, but here I was fawning over the fact that he'd said the words *need* and *you* in the same sentence. Ridiculous.

I did retain enough dignity to remember the main reason I'd gone after him. "Do you want to talk about what you saw out there today?" I asked, pushing the sleeves of my sweater up. "It must have been hard, so if you need to talk about it..."

Gabriel shifted away from me, out of the circle of light the dim bulb provided. "No," he said. He was firm, but not rude as he'd been earlier. "I'm fine."

"Maggie has a point," I said, and the silhouette of his head whipped in my direction. "You shouldn't carry this weight alone when you have people willing to help. I understand if you don't want to burden John and Maggie, but you should be able to talk to someone. And I'm happy to listen."

He remained silent. I thought I'd overstepped my bounds and that he was going to close up on me again, that he was going to push me away, but then his deep voice eased into the quiet of the room.

"I'm used to dead bodies, okay?" he started. "I know that sounds weird, but I'm a doctor. I've dissected cadavers, and I've seen things in the emergency room that would make most people snap. I've gotten used to death. But dragging those two guys deep into the woods, hiding them under mounds of snow...I've lost patients before and had to deal with it, but that was completely different than willfully taking a life. I just saw John bleeding and that guy on top of you, and—"

"You saved us," I said. The words came out soft and low, touched by the awe of acknowledging this horrible bond we shared. "I know it's hard to deal with, but you acted on instinct and you did the right thing. Those men wanted to hurt us. The look on that guy's face when he got me on the ground was terrifying. He was enjoying himself. It was more than a need for supplies." I wrapped my arms around my middle, trying to hide the shudder.

Gabriel clenched his jaw. "I don't want to be pardoned," he said. His voice was raw, but not angry. "I'd do it again in a heartbeat. But knowing that didn't make dealing with their bodies any easier. It made it worse, actually."

He went back to tallying cans, ending the conversation, and I decided not to push. I eventually kneeled beside him, checking what was in the jars that lined the bottom shelf. Green beans. As I inspected each jar, not knowing what I was looking for but mimicking Gabriel's actions, the immensity of his words hit me. He'd kill again, even though it was causing him so much pain. He'd do it for John. And for me. I gripped a jar tightly and looked up at him. From this angle, I could see that his brow was still drawn in worry. There was something else.

"So you didn't find anything on them?" I thought he'd have said something to his siblings, but the long look he'd given me in the kitchen had been disquieting. "Did you see my baseball bat, maybe?"

"Nope, there was no bat. That's the thing," he said, and then ran a hand through his hair in agitation. "Their pockets were empty. They'd been turned out. I didn't touch their stuff, and I didn't see you do it either."

I looked at him blankly, my mind teetering on understanding but not quite able to surmount the fear of acknowledging what his words meant.

"There was a set of footprints there that didn't belong to either of us," he continued, and the words sent an icy shiver of fear down my spine. I jumped to my feet, heartbeat thudding in my ears as all the terrible possibilities spiraled out in front of me. If people had found the bodies, they could find us. I remembered how quiet it had been outside the house earlier that morning. Anyone could have been hiding in that silence, watching and waiting to attack. I suddenly understood the tactics of the armadillo; I wished I could curl into the safety of myself until any threat passed. But nowhere was safe, and I had more than myself to worry about.

Gabriel went on, stepping closer to me as he spoke. "After I buried the bodies, I followed the new set of prints for a while, and they tapered off into some thick underbrush. They didn't seem to come toward the house." I picked up his unspoken worry. *But they could have already walked in our footsteps so as not to create a new trail.* He sighed deeply. "I tried to erase the trail that leads back here, though, using some tree branches. That's what took me so long. Anyway, whoever made those footprints took everything those men had. If there was any evidence of contact with my parents, it's long gone."

He took another step, one that left him close enough that I could feel his presence as much as I could see it. He eclipsed the lightbulb, the lean musculature of his body silhouetted from behind. I should have felt caged in by him, given my panic, but I felt sheltered instead. The tightness in my chest eased just the slightest bit as I leaned closer to his warmth, seeking comfort. He leaned in, too, and I realized he needed the same from me.

"Thanks for doing so much to protect us. I'm sorry you didn't find anything, Gabriel." I wasn't good at this being gentle and reassuring shit. I wished there was something I could *do* to take away the pain of his parents' disappearance, or to repay him for all that he'd done.

"I'm not sorry," he said. "That means there's still hope. I'm more worried about whoever was prowling around the bodies. I don't think they'll come this way, especially since they know we have a gun and we've killed, but it's still a problem."

"Jesus," I whispered, clenching my hands convulsively as the bubble of safety around our cabin started to burst.

"What are we going to do if someone shows up here?" I wondered if we would have to leave, dreading another trek into the brutal winter landscape. Pinpricks of panic beat a tattoo over my scalp and neck as I realized we had nowhere to go.

"I'll handle them. We'll handle them," Gabriel said in that deep, reassuring tone. I shouldn't have been comforted by mere words, but there was something about his confidence that made it hard to resist. A small smile that I knew was for my benefit played on his lips. "I don't think the risk is much higher than it's been since this whole shitstorm started. There was always a chance of someone trying to get in. We'll just need to be extra vigilant."

His fingers clasped my elbow in reassurance, and I felt just a bit of my sense of stability and safety return. He seemed reticent, as if he wanted to say something else.

"What?" I prodded, placing my hand lightly on his chest out of some innate need to comfort him through touch, as he had me.

His body was rigid with tension beneath his shirt; I looked down to see that his free hand was unconsciously balled into a fist. A sudden burst of tenderness for him bloomed within me at the sight of it. How had he managed to seem so cool during dinner with the weight of his own small world on his shoulders? How was he assuaging my fears while surely battling so many of his own?

"Do you think I should let John and Maggie know why I went out there?" he asked. "You were right. Chances are those guys had nothing to do with my parents. But I feel horrible keeping it from them. I'd want to know."

I thought of Maggie's complaint about Gabriel not telling her anything. "I don't know. You have to make that decision, but think about how you'd feel if you were in their shoes. You didn't find anything, so I don't know if it's worth worrying them, but whatever you decide, you should be honest with them from this point forward. You absolutely need to tell them that we have to be more wary."

"That's what I thought," he said. "I just hope I'm making the right decisions. It really was dumb of me to go out there on my own. They were right to be pissed at me."

"I was pissed, too," I said. The newborn tenderness throbbed painfully in my chest at the admission. I splayed my hand on his chest, feeling the play of muscles beneath my palm. "I told you not to go alone. I would've gone with you. There was someone else out there! They could have had weapons—they could have hurt you—and no one would have been there to help because you were too stubborn to confide in anyone. You can't do something like that again, Gabriel."

I only stopped my tirade because I needed to take in air. Anger, desire, fear and confusion were wreaking havoc on my emotions. I didn't know whether I wanted to hug him for trying to protect us all or hit him for putting himself into so much danger—danger that had seemed abstract until the enormity of what could have happened to him played out in my mind.

"Why would you have gone with me?" he asked quietly, his fingers slipping from their light grip on my elbow to encircle my forearm. I thought it was a trick of the dim lighting, but his hooded eyes seemed warmer as they gazed into mine, like spun honey. I wondered if he tasted of honey as well, and a spark of anticipation flared low in my belly.

"Because you should have had someone to watch your back out there," I said. My words came out low and husky, as if they'd been filtered through the confusing ache for Gabriel that was filling that hollow in my chest. "John is still recovering, and Maggie would need at least one of her brothers to stay with her."

"Even though I was a total jerk to you, you were still going to volunteer to be the person who got my back?"

He was smiling now, and it was different from the affectionate grin I'd seen him give his siblings. This one was mischievous, sensual. Not the cat who got the cream, but one who just noticed that the milkman had left the door to his truck open. Something hot and heady welled up in me, something that needed more than a smile or a stray caress. He took a step forward, and I stood my ground. The mere millimeters of space left between us seemed to be filled with charged particles that released little bursts of pleasure as they ricocheted off me.

"Well, when you put it that way, I sound pretty dumb," I admitted. "What can I say? You give one hell of a massage."

He laughed. My hand was still against his chest, and

the sensation of his mirth vibrated up my arm, quickening my breath. My body was receptive to his every motion, and for a brief moment I knew what the fly felt as the spider slowly approached from across the web. The moment was both drawn out and moving far too fast.

"Seriously, though, you saved my life," I said, hoping he couldn't hear the hitch in my breathing that his proximity caused. "Isn't there some Korean adage that says if someone saves your life, it belongs to them? I owe you."

"That's a Chinese proverb, not Korean, smart-ass," he said, his fingertips feathering over the bare skin of my forearm. "And I think the actual phrase is 'If you save someone's life, you're responsible for it.' But your version means less work for me, among other things, so I'm willing to roll with it. You *are* saying that you belong to me now, right?"

It was hard to focus on his words with the pleasant friction he was creating providing such a distraction, but even without paying attention I sensed that something had shifted between us. The air around us seemed to throb with energy synced to my rising pulse. Gabriel reached out with his free hand and traced a finger down my temple and the curve of my neck, leaving a tingle in its wake.

"That's not exactly what I meant," I said, my breath catching as he pulled me flush against him. Lean and hard, Gabriel pressed all up the front of me—I don't know what I'd expected when I'd come down to the cellar, but it hadn't been this. Not in my wildest imagination could I have imagined this flirty, brazenly sexual side of Gabriel's personality, or that it would be directed at me. I couldn't possibly have conjured how feeling each delineated ab muscle flex against my stomach as he spoke would start a sharp, sweet ache at my core. I'd never been happier to have such a limited imagination.

"That's too bad," he said. "Because although I've been trying to resist it, the idea of my own personal Arden is pretty appealing right now."

"Well, I guess I'm willing to roll with it, too," I said. Unable to fight the momentum of our encounter, and not even wanting to, I tipped up toward him on my toes just as he angled his head and swooped down, his lips crashing into mine. "Ouch. You need to work on your technique, Dr. Seong," I said, but I was smiling.

"Sorry," he muttered and pressed his lips to mine, soft as a whisper, as if trying to balance out our first attempt. His lips were firm and smooth, and when they moved over mine I let out a whimper that would have been embarrassing if there had been room for any sensation other than desire.

Gabriel smiled against my mouth. He pulled me into his arms and deepened the kiss, his tongue gently flicking across my lips until I granted him entrance. He tasted of the stew we'd eaten for dinner, warm and savory and spicy. I had guessed he would be skilled with his tongue, and he proved my guess right. He guided the kiss from tender and exploratory to deep and all-consuming with a finesse I'd never experienced before, and I had kissed a lot of toads. I followed his lead without hesitation. Kissing had always seemed like a warm-up with other guys, but with Gabriel it felt like a main event. A thrill welled up in me at each stroke of his tongue, and when he nipped at my bottom lip, it sent a bolt of electric pleasure straight to my core.

My hand was still pressed against his chest and I clutched at him, gathering his shirt in my fist so I could pull him down and bring his seeking mouth closer to mine. My other hand slid into his thick hair. I dragged my fingertips down the smooth skin of his neck, and he groaned into my mouth. I lost track of everything but our kiss, of his hands moving over my body.

His kiss was spurred by a hunger that matched my own, an outpouring of desire fueled not only by lust, but by a mutual helplessness. I didn't know what had caused the world as I knew it to shut down, but I knew that pressed against me was a man whose voice made me tremble, even when I wanted to punch him. I knew that the strong arms gathering me close belonged to someone who wanted to protect me, and those he loved.

My neck started to ache from holding my awkward stance for so long. I threw both arms about his neck in an effort to bring him down to my level, but he pulled away from me.

"Shit, did I hurt your back?" he asked, his voice husky with desire and concern as he ran his hands soothingly over my back and shoulders.

"Do I get another massage if I say yes?" I asked, reaching up to pull at him again. He was too far away now, and my senses craved the heat and the taste of him, the feel of his body against mine.

He gripped my hips through my sweatshirt and lifted me. I wrapped my legs around his waist without hesitation, and his hands slid down to cup my ass. I could feel the delicious pressure of him pulsing against me, the thin material of my leggings sliding over his jeans. He rocked against me, just a little, and an eddy of pleasure swirled through me, thrilling me from head to toe.

"That's better," he whispered harshly as he kissed his way down my jaw to the sensitive spot under my ear. I tried to swallow the soft moans he was pulling out of me, but he heard them anyway. I felt his twitch of excitement at the juncture where I was pressed against him. I moved my hips forward, adding more pressure, gasping as his erection slid against my sensitive nub once and then again, fueling a delicious heat that spread from my belly to my breasts.

"You have no idea how hard it was for me to apply that balm yesterday. You kept making the sexiest noises." He tugged my head back by the braids, locking it in place. The motion was gentle, but I could feel the constrained eagerness in the movement, and something dark and hot inside me responded. The desire for him to touch me pulsed at my core in a mad rhythm.

He pressed butterfly kisses along my jaw before moving his mouth down to my neck. His teeth grazed my skin, and I bucked against him, arching my back to better expose myself to his soft lips and to press myself more firmly against the hard length of him. He nipped and sucked at the hollow of my neck, his tongue twirling over my collarbone. Pleasure effervesced through me, spreading from my extremities and moving inward, meeting with a clenching ache in my channel. His teasing was driving me crazy and he didn't seem as if he was going to stop anytime soon; Gabriel was a thorough man.

"I tried to be quiet." I rolled my head away from his hand to free my hair from his grip and leaned in close to his ear. "But you felt so damn good that I couldn't help myself. Much like right now."

I licked at the strong line of his neck, savoring the slightly salty flavor of his skin and wondering what the rest of him tasted like. My mouth latched on to the juncture of his neck and shoulder and lingered there when I felt his enthusiastic response growing against me. His fingers flexed against my ass, and I knew he was restraining himself. There was something hot and urgent building inside me, though, and I needed him to release it.

I sucked harder.

"Kiss me again," he ordered in a ragged voice and I did, reveling in the slide of his lips against mine, the warmth of his mouth as we learned each other's rhythms. I could feel his heart beating rapidly when I pressed my hard nipples against his chest and kissed him deeper, wanting to explore every facet of him.

"Gabriel!" Maggie's voice sounded from the doorway to the cellar.

I nearly jumped off him in my surprise, but he held on, giving me a lingering kiss as he lowered me to the floor. My body slid against his during my descent, the contact making me want to clamber back up.

"What's up, Mag?" he answered in a calm tone, as if he hadn't just almost gotten me off with kisses alone. His eyes were on me but his expression was unreadable.

"Let me know what the supplies are looking like so I can plan tomorrow's dinner. I *can* plan dinner for us, right?"

While I was happy that Maggie was testing her new boundaries with her brother, she had very inopportune timing. My body thrummed with desire. I wanted more. I *needed* to taste him again. But then the logic synapses in my brain, which had temporarily been deadened by Gabriel's drugging kisses, started sparking again.

What was I doing? I couldn't get hot and heavy with John's temperamental older brother. Kissing him had felt so right, but starting a *thing* with someone I may be stuck with indefinitely during a possible apocalypse was probably not the best idea.

"Of course you can," he called up to her, and ran a hand through his wavy hair to push the disheveled strands back into place. The sound of her walking away seemed exceptionally loud, even though I hadn't heard anything of her approach. "I should finish this up," he said to me. "One of the cons of appointing yourself Fearless Leader is you have to make good on your promises."

"Only if you're good at what you do," I said, my

reathy voice making me feel like a fool. I was still a little
ight-headed from our activities and decided my energies
would best be channeled doing something to help the household. Focusing on mundane tasks seemed like a good way
stop thinking about Gabriel's hands tugging me against him.
"I'm going to go see what I can do to help upstairs."

He picked up his pen and notebook and turned back
to his inventory. I'd expected at least a "see you later." None
seemed forthcoming, so I made my way to the stairs.

He waited until I reached the bottom step to call out
my name. I planned to keep walking—instead I stopped and
turned as if compelled. His back was to me, but he spoke
in that sure, authoritative voice that sent a tremor straight
through me.

"It's really not a good idea for us to get involved, and
we probably shouldn't let something like this happen again,"
he said baldly. Although I'd just thought the same thing, his
words still stung.

He turned his head to me then, and even in the dim
light I could see that desire burned in his eyes. Desire for me.
My skin tingled under his gaze. It was as if he'd left behind
some trace of himself with his fingers, lips and tongue and
now he could caress me with just a look.

"Good ideas be damned. Next time, if you want there
to be a next time, I'm not stopping until I make you scream."

Something deep within me tightened at the thought of
him driving into me.

"I'm holding you to that, Dr. Seong," I said, starting up the steps before I did something stupid like rip his clothes off. "But keep in mind that I might make you scream first."

His voice drifted up the stairs after me. "That wouldn't surprise me at all."

9

The next few days passed at a maddeningly slow pace. We received no news from the outside world, there was no update on the elder Seongs' whereabouts and there was very little work to do in a house with four restless people running from their own thoughts.

The boredom was bad, but the worst side effect of our new lives in the era of the unknown was the lack of privacy. With all of us drifting aimlessly through the house with no set schedule, Gabriel and I hadn't had a moment alone since the interlude in the cellar. Every time we stumbled upon each other in the kitchen or hallway, either John or Maggie would pop up, oblivious that they were engaging in massive levels of cockblocking.

As disappointing as it was for my libido, on some level I appreciated the unasked-for chaperones and unintended sexual sabotage. Making out with Gabriel had been hot as hell, and I wanted more of that, but our lack of alone time meant that instead of just jumping on each other and sucking face, we actually had to get to know each other.

I kept waiting for him to say something that would render him completely unattractive to me, like a revelation that *Atlas Shrugged* was his favorite novel or that he enjoyed eating belly button lint. Instead, I learned that the only time he'd ever been reprimanded in school was for decking some jerk who'd harassed John for weeks, and that he spent his time between shifts—the time when he couldn't force himself to sleep—reading to patients in the children's oncology ward. Was he kidding me with this shit? He wasn't perfect, but the anecdotes from his siblings and our own interactions proved one thing to be true: resistance was futile. The better I got to know him, the more I wanted him. That wasn't usually how things worked out for me, and it was new and frightening territory.

Trying to make the most of my time, I spent hours working with Maggie on her guitar playing. I pushed her until her fingers bled, but it gave us both something to focus on besides the fact that life without Wi-Fi sucked. In addition to being a handy diversion, it was kind of fun having to remember how to play songs without the benefit of prewritten tabs and chord progressions at our fingertips.

"That was close, but you're letting your brain get

ahead of your fingers," I said one afternoon, readjusting Maggie's fingers on the frets of her guitar. "You have to play slowly before you really learn a song. It's not going to sound perfect the first few times, and rushing doesn't help."

"You've told me that like five times already," she griped.

"Okay, enough of that for the day," John announced as he ran into the living room and snatched the guitar out of Maggie's hands. There was only so long we could play before driving the Seong men up the wall, and apparently that limit had been reached. I tried to grab it back, but he jumped away from me and held it toward the fireplace.

"Don't think I won't," he said. "We're running low on kindling and this would kill two birds with one stone."

"You're such a jerk," Maggie growled, not deigning to chase after him.

I picked up an old magazine and ignored him, and he glumly returned the guitar to his sister.

"You girls are no fun," he said.

"We're women, John, not girls," Maggie said, and I smiled. I was rubbing off on her, it seemed.

"You're not a woman," Gabriel said as he strode into the room, bringing a blast of heat with him that seemed to affect only me. "And if any guy tries to tell you otherwise, introduce him to me and I'll set him straight."

"Ugh, both of you are jerks!" Maggie grabbed her guitar and stomped out of the room. A few moments later, her door slammed.

"I thought she'd be good for at least another ten minutes of harassment. Now who are we going to antagonize?" John asked before turning his gaze toward me.

"Don't even think about it, buddy," I said. "I'll break you over my knee and throw you on the woodpile."

John picked up the metal fire poker and pointed it in my direction. I pretended to lunge at him, and he flinched, dropping the poker and narrowly avoiding stabbing himself in the foot. Gabriel laughed, and I tried the same move on him, but he didn't even blink. He simply rocked back in his chair and crooked a finger in my direction.

"Bring it on."

I knew he was joking, but his voice made me press my thighs together even when he was being a jerk. Actual flirtation brought on the urge to jump into his lap. My cheeks blazed and I looked away quickly.

"I always lost the flinching game when we were kids." John looked dejected, as if this was high on his list of regrets. "But I was really good at hide-and-seek. I think I've only been found once in twenty-four years. That has to be some kind of record."

"Longest time spent hiding in the closet?" Gabriel

quipped. When John gave him an unamused stare, he threw up his hands. "Hey, you set them up, I knock them down."

"I liked you better before you developed a sense of humor," John said, pressing a hand to his chest and glaring at Gabriel in disdain.

"I've never really played hide-and-seek before," I said with faux casualness. "Maybe a couple of times when I visited some cousins. When your parents are almost old enough to be your grandparents and you're an only child, you spend a lot of time watching public television and going for quiet strolls in the park. I can quote every episode of *Miss Marple*, though, so I have no regrets."

I'd always dreamed of having brothers and sisters, a ready-made group of friends who would love you no matter what. Of course, it wasn't always so simple; spending time with John, Gabriel and Maggie had illustrated that well enough. But the ease they had with each other, even when they argued, sometimes made me so envious of the little things they took for granted.

"And here I thought I knew you, yet I never would have guessed that you'd led such a deprived childhood," John said. "Did your parents feed you gruel for dinner? Were the dust bunnies under the bed your only friends?"

I shot him a glare.

"Well, there's no time like the present," Gabriel said, standing and striding to the wall. He crossed his arms against the wood paneling and rested his forehead on them. I tried not to stare at his ass, outlined by the clinging material of his sweatpants. They didn't say "juicy" across the back, probably because that would have been redundant. "I'm going to count to one hundred. You guys go hide."

"Seriously?" I leaned forward in my seat. Hide-and-seek was a kid's game, and nothing I had learned about Gabriel indicated he was into frivolous wastes of time.

He shot an annoyed look at me over his shoulder. "You got anything better to do, Arden? *One, two—*"

I looked over at John, who was grinning like a fool. Just like that, we were five years old again, scrambling out of our seats and tearing through the hall, bumping into each other while we tried to navigate who would claim what part of the house for their hiding spot. I felt giddily happy as I pushed past John and rushed up the stairs.

Maggie's door opened.

"We're playing hide-and-seek!" I whispered. She shook her head in teenaged disgust and closed the door in my face. Undeterred, I continued on and opened a door to a room I hadn't been in before. As soon as I did, I realized I wouldn't be hiding there. I would abide by the rules of every childhood game—the parents' bedroom was off-limits.

I crept down the hall, Gabriel's booming voice alerting me that I didn't have very much time left. I had a sudden memory of the last time I'd played the game: me stumbling in a blind panic and eventually hiding behind a coat tree. I'd sucked at hide-and-seek, which was probably the real reason I hadn't played.

"Ninety-three! Ninety-four!"

How had the time passed so quickly? It'd been going slow as molasses all day. In a complete state of panic, I jumped into the bathroom, leaving the door open just a crack to throw Gabriel off my trail. No sane person would leave the door to their hiding spot open, would they? I congratulated myself for my craftiness and scanned the bathroom for a good place to stash myself.

I considered jumping into the bathtub and pulling the shower curtain, but that was way too easy. A large bathrobe hung from a hook on the wall, its hem hovering just over the floor.

Jackpot, I thought as I slid behind the wall of fluffy terry cloth. I felt a bit foolish in the silence that rang through the house after Gabriel stopped counting, but only because of the anticipation that thrummed through my body. The object of the game was to avoid detection, but my heart beat rapidly at the fact that Gabriel was searching for me and at the thought of what could happen if he found me.

I had no idea how long I hid under the robe— it seemed as though I spent a century straining to hear the creak of stairs or some other sound that would indicate that Gabriel was near. I was starting to chide myself for expecting anything more than an afternoon of fun when I heard the hushed glide of the bathroom door opening. And then the click of it closing and locking.

He couldn't know I'm in here. I willed my heart to stop beating so loudly and my breath to come more quietly. *You're probably about to be subjected to someone's post-kimchi intestinal distress.*

I thought about revealing myself, but I could feel Gabriel's presence when he moved in front of me. I knew it was him—my nipples hardened and my sex tightened like some kind of erotic emergency alert system. It was no surprise when the robe was lifted and he stood before me, his mouth curved in a triumphant grin.

"Well, what do we have here?" His gaze was intense as he looked down at me, and I realized I had pressed myself back against the tiles like some unlucky sheep that had been cornered by the big bad wolf.

We were finally alone.

Something hot and primeval surged through me as he dropped the robe over the edge of the tub and lowered himself onto it, sitting with his legs wide.

He didn't say a word, but his eyes communicated well enough. Hunger. Desire. Need. My body thrilled with mirrored responses, and I stepped between his legs as if he'd commanded me to. He placed his hand against the small of my back and pulled me close to him, and just like that, nothing else mattered. There was no need for foreplay or teasing—we had endured days of that already. There was only this stolen moment together, away from family and friends, taking what comfort we could from each other.

My fears for the future disappeared with the whisper of his hand sliding under my shirt and caressing my skin. The uncertainty about my parents' fate faded into the background as my fingers raked through his thick hair. The fact that when and if life went back to normal was completely out of our control didn't matter when our mouths met in a desperate tangle of tongues.

His hands skimmed up my torso, his rough palms smoothing over my waist and stomach. When he moved them up to cup my breasts, I deeply regretted my decision to wear a bra that morning. But his questing fingers wouldn't be denied, and he tugged the cups down to expose my pebbled nipples to his touch. I gasped into his mouth as he rubbed his fingertips over them, sending waves of pleasure pulsing through me. I pushed my chest forward into his hands, needing more than the languid strokes he was teasing me with.

"Fuck, Arden." His whisper was harsh against my lips, but he got my message—he didn't stop. He pinched at the hardened peaks, his groan matching my sharp gasp. His hands dipped down to grab the edge of my shirt and raise it, and then his tongue was circling over my breast, teeth scraping over my areola as he nipped and sucked.

Wild, wicked sensation slashed through my body and I fought to stay quiet, biting my lip to keep from moaning aloud. There was something thrilling about not being able to make a sound. It provided a signal boost that amplified each warm passage of his tongue over my pebbled breasts. Gabriel felt the thrill, too, it seemed, since he was doing his damnedest to make me break my silence.

His hand drifted to the waistline of my pants and his gaze locked with mine, asking permission. I wanted to say yes, but before I got the chance, reality intruded on our hedonistic escape once again. A loud noise from outside made us both freeze in place and reduced my ardor to cold ash. I knew we were both thinking the same thing: *this is it. Someone's come for us.*

We scrambled from the bathroom and down the hall, bumping into Maggie when she came flying out of her room. She gave me a look when I tugged at my bra, adjusting it through my shirt, but fear won out over curiosity as we raced down the stairs.

There was another crash from outside as we touched down in the foyer, and my blood ran cold at the imagined hordes encroaching upon our safe haven. I didn't want to fight, but when I looked at Maggie's wan face, I knew I'd rip the throat out of the first person who tried to get through that door.

We stood tensed, listening for something that would

indicate what kind of danger awaited us outside. Finally, Maggie began to advance, arm outstretched as if she was ready to swing the door open and let in whoever lurked on the other side.

Gabriel grabbed for her and shook his head, but she tugged free and pointed toward the peephole in the door. Without waiting for his permission, she ran and peeked through.

"Oh my God," she said, turning and sagging against the door.

"What is it?" Gabriel growled.

"Deer." She unlocked the door and flung it open. "The freaking mother lode of deer."

Dozens of deer filled the woods surrounding the house. They milled about, foraging for food and generally paying us no mind. Fawns cantered around their parents' hooves, and a four-point buck used his antlers to shake snow from a bush before nibbling on it.

"What the fuck? Is this normal?" I asked. I didn't consider myself a city girl, but this was above and beyond anything I'd ever seen.

"I don't think so," Maggie said. "But usually they're stuck in one place unless they want to get run over trying to cross the highway. Maybe they've already started adapting to life without us humans messing up the natural order."

"You know, you're not making this less scary," I sniped, staring out at the herd.

"Hey, you asked," she said, shutting and locking the door. I glanced at Gabriel, who was deep in thought.

"At least we have an alternate food source nearby if they don't travel too far," he said, because of course that was what he'd say. "Once there's room in the freezer, we'll go hunting."

"If things aren't back to normal by then," I added, although no part of me believed that normal would be happening anytime soon.

John strolled into the hallway then, yawning widely before leaning on the banister. "I fell asleep in my hiding spot. What did I miss? Did Gabriel find you, Arden?"

Oh he found me, all right.

"Your hide-and-seek champion record is safe," I hedged, hoping I wasn't blushing too hard. "And you missed a pack of rabid deer surrounding the house and scaring the shit out of us."

John looked through the peephole and shuddered dramatically. "Do you think they're Russian spy deer?"

The keening cry of a doe came from outside, as if in answer.

"Canadian," I said, hoping to lighten the mood.

A deer cried out again, sounding startlingly like a human scream.

"Let's hope so," Gabriel said, coming to stand beside me. "At least they'll be polite when they eat our faces off."

I burst out laughing, leaning into him a bit. Just like that, I wasn't so afraid anymore.

10

"Kids in Europe start drinking when they're, like, ten," Maggie said when John passed her over while pouring rice wine at dinner that night. We were all still a little shaken up by the great deer invasion of early afternoon, and those of us over the age of twenty-one handled it like adults— by purposefully destroying brain cells.

"Send me a postcard from Europe when you arrive," John said, placing the bottle down on the wooden table.

Maggie took a sip of her diet soda and looked around the table conspiratorially. "We should do something tomorrow night."

"Something like what?" Gabriel asked. His gaze flicked to my face for a second, and then back down to his food. He hadn't spoken to me since we'd sat down at the table, but I kept catching him looking at me. I played it cool, but my stomach fluttered each time I caught his searing gaze directed at me, however briefly. I couldn't stop thinking of his mouth and hands on me and wondered if he was having the same problem.

"Like a game night," Maggie said.

"That sounds like fun," Gabriel said. "What kind of games?" I could see from the crease in his brow that he was already catastrophizing, as if she was a toddler and not a teen. "Like, are you talking a scavenger hunt in the woods or board games?"

His helicopter brothering made sense. Although we'd had several talks about being more vigilant, he hadn't told John and Maggie about the footprints near the bodies to my knowledge. A plan that involved heading into the woods wouldn't be the craziest thing for a teenager trapped in a house with her annoying siblings to come up with.

"A casino night," Maggie said, brightening up as if selling us on the concept. Gabriel relaxed a bit. "Mom and Dad have a poker set, with chips and everything. It could be fun."

"You know how to play poker?" I asked.

"I'm Korean," she said, the "duh" heavily implied by her tone.

"I taught her when she was still in diapers," John corrected, although he was smiling at his sister in adoration.

"And I want to make dinner again, since my Spam casserole didn't turn out so great the other night. I need a pen and paper, so I can make an itinerary for tomorrow," she said excitedly, jumping up from the table.

"Do you really need to—" Gabriel started, but I interrupted him.

"Go get the pen and paper so you can write down everything you'll need. We can help you plan your dinner menu too," I said to Maggie.

He gave me a confused look, but instead of arguing he stood and started collecting the empty dishes.

When Maggie returned, she sat and wrote "Casino Night in Purgatory" in loopy letters at the top of a piece of paper. "We were reading Dante in English class," she explained when we groused about the title.

She then proceeded to make a tight schedule of every moment between six and nine o'clock the next night, happily letting everyone know what games they'd be enjoying at what time.

As I watched her preen over her schedule, which was about the only thing she had control over at the moment, I mused that she was much more like Gabriel than she thought.

"That looks great, Maggie," I said cheerfully. I wanted to support her, but it was also genuinely nice to have something fun to look forward to.

"Awesome. Can I have a glass of sake to celebrate?" she said, testing her new limits.

"Sure," John said.

"Hell no," Gabriel growled, snatching the bottle from the table.

Maggie huffed, annoyed that her gambit hadn't worked but apparently unsurprised. "Whatever. I'm going to go see if I can find something for you guys to wear. Mom and Dad have some cool stuff in their room."

"Oh, please no," John said. "I've seen your millennial idea of style, and I refuse to wear an ironic T-shirt or anything bedazzled."

"It's casino night! You'll dress up and you'll like it," she said with mock severity.

"I'd like a feather boa, in pink, please," I said.

"And I'll take a smoking jacket," Gabriel said, trying to join in on the fun. "Just make sure the curtains are drawn while you search. There aren't blackout curtains in their room, and you don't want to make the place a beacon for whatever crazies are out there."

He said it with affection, probably just looking for something to rib his sister about and not wanting to bring up his real fears quite yet, but Maggie went stock-still at his words.

"Mom and Dad are out there, too," she said, her mood dipping from elated to sullen in an instant. "They might need a beacon to get back home. Did you ever think of that?"

I busied myself with wiping off the dishes, not wanting

to meet any of their eyes. We'd been avoiding any mention of their parents' absence over the past couple of days. John and I had spoken about it in whispers, careful not to upset the others. Gabriel had been reticent about discussing them since moving the bodies. It had been over two weeks since the Seongs had disappeared, and it couldn't be denied that things didn't look good for them.

"Mom and Dad will find a way home if they can," Gabriel said, and then used a variation of the argument that I'd thrown at him when we'd clashed. "Do you think Dad would be happy if he was walking in the woods and saw our house sticking out like a sore thumb? No. He'd be furious."

"Gabriel's right," John said, placing his hand on her shoulder lightly, as if he expected her to shrug him off. "Do you want me to help you look for outfits?"

"I want to be alone," she said, and then caught herself. "I'm sorry. It's just hard not having them here with us."

"I understand," Gabriel said. "John and I love Mom and Dad, but you live with them. You were with them every day, and them not being around is affecting you the hardest. I wish there was something I could do to bring them back."

He paused, and I held my breath.

"But there isn't," he finished, his voice cracking. "We just have to hope that they return soon, or that everything goes back to normal so we can get help searching for them."

The tension of their loss hung in the air, weighing down the silence. It hurt like hell to see them missing their parents and not being able to help. It hurt even more to think of my own parents. Had they had enough water stocked up? Had Mom re-upped on her meds, or was she down to her last pill when everything shut down? I might never know. They were so far away, clear on the opposite side of the country. There was no feasible way to reach them if things didn't return to normal at some point. Tears pressed at the back of my eyes and my throat clogged with emotion. I'd been so happy to get away from California when I'd left for college, convincing myself that my parents were only a plane ride away. One plane ride was a hell of a long walk.

"I didn't mean to snap at you. Again," Maggie said.

"It's okay, Mags," Gabriel said with a shrug. "Once you've had the chief of surgery call you an incompetent shit-face in front the entire staff, everything else is water off a duck's back."

"Did someone really call you that?" she gasped, her watery eyes wide with surprise.

"I've been called worse," he said, and then glanced my way. "I'm not always the easiest person to get along with."

Maggie rolled her eyes, yet another of the many ways she masterfully conveyed a "duh" without words, and then left the room. We could hear the stairs creaking as she climbed.

"She's holding up pretty well for someone her age," I said, still unable to meet John's or Gabriel's eyes.

"She's holding up better than I am, and I'm not even talking about the head injury," John said, flopping down on one of the kitchen chairs.

"What do you mean?" I asked.

"I mean that I feel like I'm about to go crazy. I thought when we got here everything would be better. Do you know what I wanted most?" he asked, his voice tinged with longing. "I wanted to come home and have Mom give me one of those crazy long hugs and to tell me that I needed a haircut and a boyfriend but that she loved me anyway. I wanted Dad to make fun of my jacket and get all awkward when I said something too gay for him. But that didn't happen because they decided to put themselves in danger for this Darlene person who probably wouldn't lift a pinkie to help them if the tables were turned."

"Mom and Dad wouldn't care about whether she would have helped them, and neither should you," Gabriel said. "They knew that it wasn't entirely safe when they decided to go. You don't have to like their choice, but you do have to respect it."

John grimaced and folded his arms across his chest. I'd seen him react this way before when he was close to emotional overload, and usually I was the only one there to look out for him. I wanted to go give him a noogie and bother him to take his mind off things, but this was much more serious than being depressed over work or a guy. I decided to defer to Gabriel.

"I'm going to check out the radio again to see if I can pick anything up on the different wavelengths," Gabriel said. "You're better at that stuff than I am though. Can you give me a hand?"

John stared into the distance as if he hadn't heard, but then got up to shadow Gabriel. "It must be so hard for you being the hot medically trained brother instead of the one who can work a CB radio," he griped as they left the room.

I found myself alone in the kitchen. I felt a pang for a second, but then realized that besides the time I'd spent in the bathroom, I hadn't really had much time to myself since this whole fiasco had started. Fear and uncertainty had kept John and me clinging to each other from the start, and he or Maggie or Gabriel had always been around since we'd arrived at the house.

A low fire was burning behind the hearth grate, and I curled up on the floor in front of it.

I stared at the undulating flames, following their hypnotic motion as if it was a riveting film. I'd never been able to meditate, but watching the fire writhe behind the grate helped clear my mind, which was cluttered with thoughts of parents and death and sex.

I'd thought once we arrived that everything would be simple. Although the threats of starvation and death were drastically reduced, I was still frightened and unmoored. Now that my physical safety was ensured, I had time to think, which was even more daunting than my journey here had been. What was a few days roughing it out in the cold compared to not knowing if this was just the run-up to some new and unimaginable horror? Nothing I'd seen and nothing that we'd learned since we'd arrived had provided any knowledge that could help me figure out our situation; instead, I was even more confused. In addition to my own problems and those of a scared friend, I now had a confused teenager and an inappropriate crush thrown into the mix.

I thought of the planes of Gabriel's face at the moment when we'd crashed toward each other in the cellar, our logic burned away by a sudden flare of desire. It had been as if some shift in our genetic makeup had changed polarity, bringing us together suddenly and irresistibly. Maybe it was because I'd been lost for so many weeks, but his lips against mine had felt like the sweetest homecoming. It had been different during the game of hide-and-seek though. There had been a longing that seemed both familiar and entirely new.

I closed my eyes and let the warmth of the fire soothe me. The next thing I knew, I was being hefted into the air. I awoke with a start, attributing the sensation to that strange feeling of falling that I sometimes experienced before going to sleep, but that usually didn't come with the solid warmth of Gabriel's chest.

"Thought you might be more comfortable in a bed," he said in a low voice. I could feel his lean biceps flex along one side of my body and the support of his veined forearms on the other. I released an unsteady breath and allowed myself to revel in the sensation. The house was quiet all around us; the others were in their rooms or asleep.

We were alone.

"I think you just have some creepy fetish that involves picking up little people," I said.

"Only certain little people," he said with a laugh.

The rumble of his voice in his chest reverberated through my body, and my skin prickled with desire in response. I settled more comfortably against him as he ascended the stairs. He smelled good, although I couldn't quite pinpoint the scent, and it felt too weird to describe it as "Gabriel." That was what it was though: sweat, soap and annoyingly hot doctor. I turned my head a little to breathe him in and felt the steady beat of his heart under my ear, the rise and fall of his chest. What would it be like to spend the night with him, to curl against him like this in a darkened room? And what would we do before curling up? The images that flashed in my head, combined with the memories of what his hands and mouth could do, made me flush with heat. There was no way he hadn't noticed my change in body temperature or my racing pulse. I squirmed in his arms, but he just held me tighter as I burned for him.

"Did you guys hear anything on the radio?" I asked, trying not to show my eagerness, although I already knew his answer from the fact that the house was silent around us.

"No. But I think John feels a bit better. He needed something to do, too," he said. "After watching you with Maggie, seeing how happy she was to plan something out and be in charge for a change, I realized that trying to be in control of everything wasn't helping them."

"You are wise, Fearless Leader," I said with a smile as we reached the top of the stairs. To my surprise, he stopped and placed me on my feet in front of the door to John's room, where I'd awoken earlier.

"This is your stop," he whispered.

He hadn't been talking about *his* bed. I tamped down the desire that had been welling up in me and tried to pretend my expectations weren't dashed.

"Oh. Yeah. Good night," I mumbled, but before I could flee into the room in embarrassment he reached down, cupped my face in his hands and gave me a thorough kiss that about buckled my knees.

Had kissing always felt this amazing? The sensation of his lips against mine, his probing tongue demanding entry, nearly undid me then and there as if I was some sheltered virgin. He tasted minty, as if he'd already brushed before bed. The cool of the mint and warmth of his mouth proved to be a pleasurable contrast as his tongue slicked over mine. His grip on my face was gentle, but I grasped him by both wrists to pull myself in closer. I moaned into his mouth when his tented length grazed my stomach, and he growled in return before breaking away from me.

His thumbs slid over my cheeks as he moved to release me, one grazing the sensitive skin of my kiss-bruised lips. I caught it between my teeth and flicked it with my tongue. The tremor that ran through him, the way he squeezed his eyes shut and went still from that one lash of my tongue, was the sexiest thing I'd ever seen. Molten need flowed in my veins and I itched to touch him, to feel more of him. All of him. I would have sunk to my knees in the dim hallway if he hadn't finally spoken.

"John was looking for you earlier," he said in a husky voice as he reluctantly extricated his thumb. His breaths were short, his words clipped. "And because I'm a good brother, I won't be selfish."

I had spent most of the day with John, but Gabriel was right. Just because it was possibly the end-times didn't mean I was going to become the woman who ditched her best friend for some tail.

"Of course," I said with a smirk. "Don't be so presumptuous. I was merely going to see if you needed to be tucked in."

"If you come into my bedroom, that's the absolute last thing you'd be doing," he said. His hot gaze showed he wasn't just talking a big game. Pleasure trembled over my skin from my neck to the tips of my aching breasts.

"And to think, I thought you were an uptight control freak," I mused.

"I tend to veer into the asshole lane when I'm under stress, but I'm not uptight," he said, feigning offense. "I prefer the term 'dominating.'" He looked at me for a long moment as if trying to figure something out about me. "I think you will, too," he said cockily, and turned and walked down the hall.

I could feel the huge, stupid grin plastered onto my

face as I watched him retreat. A week ago I'd been trudging toward an uncertain future, then wondering if my life would end in the middle of a snowswept field. Happiness and desire had seemed foreign, something that had been possible in the past but was just a hypothetical in this new era of confusion and isolation.

I placed a hand to my lips, thought of the way Gabriel had looked at me right before he'd moved in to kiss me. I wasn't deluding myself, but it was more than nice to have something solid to tether myself to in a world that was becoming increasingly intangible.

I reined my libido in before stepping into my shared room. A tea candle burned, allowing me to see John, who lay on his bed staring at the ceiling. His gaze briefly shifted to me and he looked so utterly lost that I stopped in my tracks. I'd seen him mope and rage and even cry once or twice, but nothing like this. I went to the bed and curled up beside him, watching the profile of his face as he resumed his inspection of the ceiling.

"John, what's wrong? Besides everything?" I asked. "Do you need me to smash anyone for you? That might be awkward, since the only other people here are your siblings and one of them is a minor...I'll still do it though."

He sputtered out a little laugh, and at the same time a tear streaked from his eye and into his hairline. My heart twisted as he dashed the tear away with the heel of his hand. I didn't consider myself maternal—babies were several rungs below teenagers on my personal "nope" scale—but in that moment I felt like I should rock him in my arms or sing him a lullaby or something. I nudged him with my elbow instead. Sometimes tough love was more effective.

He nudged me back, a bit harder than I appreciated, and released a shuddering sigh. "No need for Arden Smash time. I'm just wishing Godzilla or aliens, or at the very least a Russian dude with a crazy fur hat, would show up on the scene so we could know what's going on. Are we supposed to just live like this forever? Am I supposed to grow old in this house?"

His tears slid freely now, and I threw an arm around him, tough love be damned. His chest rose and fell jerkily as he struggled to contain his sobs. My own chest burned in empathy, but I tilted my head back to keep the tears from falling.

"I just always thought there would be time, you know? I lived my life like everything could wait until another day, but now I might spend the rest of my life waiting for a light to come on that always stays dim. If we're not going to get explanations, then someone needs to drop a damn bomb or something." He gave an angry sniffle.

I didn't know what to say. John was usually the one tasked with keeping people happy, and seeing him give in to this despair threw me. I had no answers.

"Something's gotta give eventually, John. And when it does, we'll probably wish we were back here in bed wishing that Godzilla had absconded with Mothra instead of attacking." I hoped my descent into nerdery would raise his spirits, but he wasn't taking the bait.

"Okay, then I wish this damned headache would go away, or that Gabriel had raided the supply closet at his hospital before he'd left. Getting knocked out isn't as easy-breezy as they make it look in the movies."

It hurt my heart to see my friend so despondent. "Is there anything I can do to help?" I asked, my voice pitched higher than normal as it squeaked out around the lump in my throat.

"You can save the day and put everything aright, if it's not too much trouble," he said. He settled into the mattress as the anger sapped from him.

"Oh, you want me to do that now? I was going to wait until morning, but since you're so freaking impatient..." I moved to get up, and he swatted me back down. He laughed, and the sound gave me a bit of comfort. I couldn't actually save the day, but I could still make John smile. That counted for something.

"How about you just tell me a story instead?"

A knock sounded at the door just then. It swung open to reveal Maggie, dragging her blanket behind her like a *Peanuts* character. "I had a bad dream," she said, her red-rimmed eyes proof to the severity of her nightmare. "Can I sleep in here?"

"Sure, take my bed," I said. "I was about to tell John a story. You look like you could use one too."

"You guys really need to grow up," she said, all teen-age cool as she flopped onto the other twin bed. She looked over at me expectantly.

"You're never too old for a bedtime story, child," John said. "Unfortunately, most of us don't realize that until it's too late."

"There once lived a prince named John," I began. "He ruled over Seongistan, a land that produced the studliest, most handsome men on the entire planet. All of them strove to gain his particular favor, but the prince had promised his godmother, a sexy black fairy named Arden, that he would only settle for the smartest, most humorous, most kind man in the land..."

I spun a story of conquest and adventure, eventually drawing in Maggie as the humble but badass peasant girl who helped Prince John find the man of his dreams and save the misunderstood dragon he was originally supposed to slay.

"How come Gabriel wasn't in the story?" Maggie asked around a yawn when I had given everyone their happily-ever-after. I felt my cheeks warm, but John answered for me.

"He was the dragon, silly," he said. "Don't you know your own brother?"

"Eew! I thought the dragon sounded kind of hot," she said, her sleepy voice edged with horror.

"I guess our storyteller is a little biased," John said around a yawn.

They drifted off to sleep one after the other, and

eventually I followed. I dreamed of a dragon with golden eyes curled up on the roof of the house, protecting us from all who meant to do us harm.

For the first time in weeks, I slept soundly.

11

I woke up earlier than John and Maggie. When I peeked through a crack in the boards covering the window, I could see that the sun was just rising over the tree line, limning the skeletal treetops in shades of orange and yellow. A couple of months ago I would have snapped a picture of the view and posted it online, but that wasn't a part of my reality anymore. Instead, I scanned the wooded area in my line of sight for movement or evidence that anyone had infringed upon our refuge.

I tiptoed out of the room, mindful of the sleeping siblings; they looked so peaceful in their slumber that I didn't want to be the one to wake them. I headed for the kitchen, which held the promise of instant coffee. I tried not to think of the day the coffee would run out, hoping that things would be back to normal before we had to experience that particular circle of hell.

A movement in my peripheral vision as I reached the first floor landing caused my stomach to tighten with fear, and I gasped aloud.

"It's just me," Gabriel said in a low voice. He stepped through the cellar door and headed toward the living room carrying a large black lockbox.

I followed him, my curiosity overriding my desire for caffeine.

He put the box down on the coffee table, and that was when I noticed the dull gleam of the shotgun propped against the comfy sofa. I remembered how loud it had been in the clearing, but it lay there quietly now, menace and savior rolled into one. I realized Gabriel was preparing for uninvited guests.

"There's ammo in here," he said, taking a seat on the sofa in front of the lockbox. I heard the click of small gears turning as he aligned the tumblers to the right code and popped open the lid. There were at least a dozen boxes of shells. A small handgun lay atop the bullets. "You and John will have to arm wrestle for this one," he said, as though he was talking about the last slice of pie at dessert.

"I've never used a gun before." I watched his every move as he examined the small firearm. He joked with me, but he handled the weapon with the respect of someone who actually understood what a deadly tool it was. "I don't know how to."

"Dad used to take John and me to the shooting range all the time. I wonder if Maggie knows how to shoot? I'm not giving her a gun just yet, but she might have to learn eventually if—" He stopped and placed the gun down on the table, and then cracked his knuckles. "Come sit next to me," he said. His voice had its usual commanding tone, but I could sense something else beneath it. Fear? I didn't know what it was, but I wasn't in the mood to be bossed around.

I crossed my arms and stared at him.

"Please," he added. It was still a command, but tinged with humor instead of something that frightened me.

I nodded and took a seat next to him. He ran a hand over my back, a brief movement that was more comfortable greeting than seduction, and then passed me the handgun.

"It's not loaded and there's no bullet in the chamber," he said as I took it.

It wasn't as heavy as I thought it would be. The metal was cool in my hand, and I felt a little thrill of power knowing what the weapon could do to someone who wanted to hurt us. But then an image of Blue Hat, bloody and dying, flashed in my mind, and I reminded myself there was no enjoyment to be had in this kind of power.

"Hold it like this, rest your finger here, outside the trigger guard. It should always be here until you're ready to pull the trigger so you don't shoot anyone by accident," he said, positioning my fingers on the gun.

I held the gun out in front of me, pointing it toward the empty fireplace. My shoulders were back and I closed one eye to align the sights and take aim.

"Nice," Gabriel said, surprised. "I thought you hadn't handled a gun before?"

"John forces me to play Call of Duty with him. Besides, this part seems pretty intuitive," I said, just as he repositioned my thumb.

"That hammer goes back when you shoot. Don't rest your thumb there unless you want it broken."

"Okay, maybe not completely intuitive," I quipped.

He got up and walked over to the fireplace and stood in front of it. "This is center mass. This is where you want to hit someone." He moved his hand in a circular motion over his torso. "Now, aim at me, take a deep breath and pull the trigger on the exhale."

"How about you move and I pretend you're still there and then pull the trigger?" I countered, lowering the gun and opening both eyes.

"I want you to know how it feels to take aim at a person and fire," he said. "I checked to make sure there's no ammo in there—several times. Trust me, I'm not trying to commit suicide by Arden."

I slid the safety on. I knew the gun wasn't loaded, but I still couldn't bring myself to put Gabriel in my crosshairs. What if some freak accident occurred? What if I hurt him? I remembered Blue Hat flying off me, the mist of his blood that had covered me. Except now, in my mind, it was Gabriel whose chest exploded in a cloud of red. The eyes that stared without seeing were amber instead of gray. My hands tightened around the cold steel, hard enough that my fingers started to go numb. Gabriel sighed in impatience.

"Come on, I know you've wanted to shoot me at least once since you got here," he joked. I didn't laugh.

"Why are you asking me to do this?" I asked. "Is this— Do you want me to know how you felt when you shot those men?" Tears stung my eyes at the thought that he would put me in this position as a way of getting back at me.

"No, of course not." He strode over to me and clasped my shoulders in his hands. "Arden...look. The first time I had to stitch up a patient, I messed up three times before I got it right. I had practiced for hours and hours, but I still fucked up when it came down to it, despite the fact that it was a clean slice on an easy area to sew up."

"What does that have to do with anything?" I glared up at him.

"I don't want you to freeze up if you ever have to do this in real life. Taking aim at a wall or a paper target is completely different than taking aim at a person, and that doesn't even factor in fear, shaking hands, adrenaline rushes." He held me a little tighter, and his voice was rough when he continued. "I need to know that if something happens and I'm not around that you'll be able to shoot."

His eyes were focused, intense, and I realized he was asking me to do this because he cared. Messed up as it was, warmth bloomed within me, a strange sensation that made my chest feel both drawn in and ready to burst at the same time.

Gabriel kept talking while he stepped away from me and resumed his position. "I didn't know you when I first came across that bastard on top of you, and that shook me up badly. But I know you now, and I can't deal with the thought of something like that happening again, especially if I'm not with you. Aim and shoot."

His words momentarily stunned me, but it was the look on his face that took my breath away. He grimaced as if the thought of something happening to me actually pained him. Who knew that a guy asking me to reenact a scene from a snuff film would be the most romantic thing anyone had ever done for me? Flowers had never really been my style anyway.

I pushed past the innate directive against harming another person, especially someone I cared about, took aim and squeezed the trigger. A brief wave of nausea edged into my throat, but the hollow click verified that I hadn't done any harm. I repeated the action from different stances as Gabriel stood there grinning as if I was performing a choreographed dance routine instead of shooting at him.

"Good job! You're a regular Calamity Jane," he said. When I stared at him blankly, he shook his head. "Remind me to lend you my *Sharpshooters of the Old West* book. And to challenge your history teacher to a duel."

"Sharpshooter? You can trace the path of my invisible bullets?" I pointed the gun away from him and put the safety back on.

"You had the right stance, you didn't waver and you

didn't stop shooting. There'll be kickback when the gun is loaded, but I think you can handle it. This gun shoots .22s," he said. Without warning, he pretended to lunge for me and I swung the gun up and clicked the safety off.

"Whoa. That was *so* hot," he said with a grin that I couldn't help but return.

Just then, John and Maggie walked in. Both of our heads whipped guiltily in their direction.

"What in the messed-up-roleplaying hell are you guys doing in here?" John asked, his eyes wide with mock horror. "Can you save the kinky stuff for the bedroom please? Think of the children." He pulled Maggie close to him, clamping his hand over her eyes.

I lowered the gun and burst out laughing. Gabriel looked at me with raised eyebrows, and then he was laughing too. Even though they didn't quite understand what was going on, John and Maggie were drawn into the fold, laughing as wildly as we were.

"It's not what it looks like," Gabriel said as he struggled to catch his breath.

"I hope not," Maggie said. "That would be worse than the time I found *The Joy of Sex* on Mom and Dad's nightstand."

That set us into another fit of laughter, but when it finally died down, Gabriel's explanation of why the guns were out sobered everyone's mood.

"So you think that this person who was creeping

around the bodies might show up here?" John asked when Gabriel was done recounting his morbid discovery.

Gabriel shrugged. "I don't know, but we really should be prepared for anything. We should have talked about contingency plans earlier, but I'd really hoped things wouldn't come to that."

Maggie was normally pale, but after Gabriel spoke she was positively ashen. Her lips were drawn into a thin line and her eyes were wide with worry. I put my arm around her shoulder.

"Don't worry, kid, we'll be okay. We can handle anyone that shows up." I hoped I wasn't lying to her.

She nodded, but didn't look at me.

"Are these the only weapons we have?" John asked, inspecting the shotgun like an old pro. And here I'd thought I knew everything about him.

"The only ones I could find," Gabriel said.

"I have my hatchet," John said, "but I don't really want to get that close to anyone trying to get in here."

"I have pepper spray," I said. "Unfortunately, the forager had excellent taste in baseball bats and took my slugger."

Maggie started under my arm, and I released her from my loose hold.

"You okay?" I asked. I thought she was reacting

strongly to Gabriel's revelation, but then I remembered that she was a sheltered kid. She was probably scared shitless.

"Yeah, just a little freaked out. I have something, though," she said, and darted from the room. When she returned, she was lugging a black case that was over half her height.

"Do you have an afterschool job with the mafia?" I asked. She laid the case flat, released its clasps and revealed the shiny pink compound bow nestled in the felt lining of the case.

"I tried making it to the International Archery Championship a couple of years ago," she said, lifting the bow and holding it reverently. She assumed a shooting stance that hinted at formidable skill. "I didn't get anywhere close to the top of the Junior division, but I was still pretty good."

"Oh, yeah," John drawled, looking at the ceiling as if recalling a memory.

"I didn't know that," Gabriel said, dropping his gaze to the ground.

"It's not like I actually made it or anything." Maggie placed the bow down.

There was an awkward silence, followed by the snapping latches of the case being closed.

"I don't want us to go into a state of constant terror," Gabriel said. "But I think we should make sure that we're being vigilant. No fires during the day if we can help it so no one is attracted to the smoke. We have to make sure the doors are locked and the curtains are closed. No going outside alone. I'm thinking of stringing up some old-fashioned tin-can motion detectors so we can hear if anyone is approaching."

"This is starting to feel more and more like a horror movie," I said without thinking.

"I know it's scary, but let's try to think of this as more Abbot and Costello than M. Night Shyamalan," Gabriel said.

"As long as there are no zombies," John said with a shudder. "I hate zombies."

"If this were a zombiepocalypse, I think we'd have seen some brains scattered along the road on our way here," I said.

Gabriel rolled his eyes, something he seemed to have picked up from Maggie, but John paled.

"Not funny, Arden," he said. He really wasn't kidding about hating zombies, and considering that we didn't know what was going on out there, I shouldn't push it.

"John, I think we should keep the handgun in your room," Gabriel said in his assured voice, making us all feel safe again. "I'll keep the shotgun at hand. Maggie, you can keep your bow wherever feels most comfortable to you."

"I guess I'll be on pepper spray patrol," I said glumly. I hoped we wouldn't have to use any of these weapons, but

I still resented not being assigned a good one.

"I'm sure Gabriel is willing to share his boom stick with you, Arden," John said, mischief dancing in his dark eyes. Either he'd forgiven me for my zombie remarks or he was punishing me for them.

"You really are insufferable," I said, hoping my hot cheeks weren't noticeable.

"You know, for the only non-Asian in the house, you really have been blushing a lot. Are you sneaking sips of vodka when we aren't looking?" John prodded.

Of course he'd noticed. I flung a throw pillow at him as I made my escape from the room, fleeing under the ruse of retrieving my pepper spray. I still didn't know what to make of Gabriel's behavior. He was a man who was serious about protecting those he cared deeply about, and he'd just made it very clear that he wanted to protect me. He'd obviously spent enough time thinking about it that he'd been driven to act on it. And he hadn't tried to pull any alpha male bullshit either. Instead, he'd taught me to defend myself.

That warm feeling swirled in my stomach as I thought of him standing before me, demanding that I shoot at him. It may have been twisted, but if John and Maggie hadn't walked in I would have jumped him then and there, firearms be damned.

12

The rest of the day leading up to casino night went by excruciatingly slow. I was already somewhat acclimated to not knowing the exact time. It was not having anything to do to kill said time that was excruciating. Before, I could have entertained myself by playing games on my smartphone, or reading celebrity gossip on one of the various blogs I followed. I could have immersed myself in international news, or instant-messaged a friend across the country. Now, my entire world was confined to this cabin and the people in it.

No wonder people used to go to bed so early back in the day. Then again, retiring early might not be too bad if Gabriel was waiting between the sheets for me. Those kinds of thoughts definitely didn't help me in the nervous energy department.

I was too restless to enjoy reading. The house had

been cleaned and recleaned by each of us, making any further attempts overkill. I tried to force an additional guitar lesson on Maggie, but she was busy planning the menu and obsessing over casino night, and she soundly rejected any offers of help.

"Are you kidding me?" she asked. "As soon as I'm done, I'm going to be just as bored as you are. Find your own project!"

Frustrated, I stomped up the steps into John's room, threw myself on my bed and flailed around in imitation of a toddler's tantrum. John, who was sitting cross-legged on his bed and closely studying some kind of chart, didn't even look up at me. He was fully in the nerd zone, which was a strange sight because his face wasn't illuminated by the glow of a computer screen, like when he went down the rabbit hole of internet information searching. He had apparently found other ways to geek out.

I thought about bounding onto his bed and harassing him—not out of spite, but for lack of anything better to do—but decided against it. He was entitled to his own time to relax without being used as a distraction from my thoughts.

My lack of activity was driving me batty for a variety of reasons, but mostly because my restless mind kept circling back to one thought: Gabriel. How hot he was, how he made me laugh, how good his body felt against mine. Against all reason, and despite our decidedly unfriendly first encounters, I was in the midst of a full-blown crush. That would have been fine in the normal world, but in the enclosed snow globe of the Seong cabin, there was no escaping it.

I knew that my attraction to him was genuine, but cabin fever seemed to be amplifying the sensation, blowing it up to the point of fixation, which just wasn't my style. I wanted his comfort and his heat and his friendship, but I didn't want to lose any more of myself than I already had.

"Why don't you do some jumping jacks or something instead of lying there overthinking things," John said. I glanced at him. He picked up a cardboard circle covered with small numbers and fiddled with it. The device was actually a moving wheel that made calculations of some sort.

"I was thinking about what's going to happen if we run out of food," I lied, and then felt even worse because I hadn't been and it was something we needed to take into consideration.

"No, you weren't. You were finding some reason to wriggle out of the fact that you like my brother."

"Okay, have you developed some post–head injury psychic powers?" I asked, pushing up on my elbows. I kind of hoped he had. Maybe then we would finally know what was going on.

"Right now I'm using this star finder wheel to determine exactly what constellations will be above us today. Because the night sky doesn't change much, I know where Saturn will be, and Mars and Orion," he said. He glanced at me and arched a brow. "You're just as predictable. This moping and navel-gazing usually precedes the 'I just don't think he's right for me' speech you use to justify your independent woman hang-up."

Ouch. Someone had been paying close attention to my dating habits over the past few years, and it certainly wasn't me. I wanted to be mad, but I couldn't deny what he said. Not a word of it.

"What's wrong with not wanting to be dependent on a man?" It was wonderful to know that Gabriel wanted to keep me safe, but it felt like giving something up to admit that I didn't want to do everything on my own.

"Nothing's wrong with that." The way he said the words, a disdainful drawl, indicated he thought otherwise. He made an adjustment to his star wheel, and then turned an exasperated gaze in my direction. "But you're not Miss Independence—you're a human who enjoys affection. And Gabriel isn't just another one of your hapless dates—he's my brother. I love you, and I have no problem with anything happening between you two, so I'll say this nicely. Don't fuck with my brother's emotions."

My stomach lurched. "Weren't you the one encouraging me to have sweaty monkey sex with him?"

"Yes, but that was then. Now I see the way he looks at you, and the way you look at him. And then I see you in here trying to talk yourself out of it."

I crossed my arms over my chest. "I wouldn't hurt your brother," I said. "Let's keep it real. He'd be the one to end up hurting me. That's how these things work with hot doctors, right?"

John stopped fiddling with his star wheel. "Arden, it would be really sad if even the freaking apocalypse couldn't get you to drop your defenses and let someone in. I've never seen Gabriel react to someone quite the way he does to you. He can be an overbearing jerk, but I can tell you from experience that he's a sensitive overbearing jerk."

John's voice wasn't harsh; however, for him to say anything at all meant he was really worried.

"I guess I *am* pretty predictable," I admitted. I dropped my head back onto my pillow.

"I've seen enough guys leaving our apartment with their heads hung low to know your modus operandi. But most of those guys were losers, to be honest. Especially that guy who kept drinking my Diet Coke. He needed to go."

"Which guys weren't losers?" I asked hesitantly. Diet Coke Thief aside, I'd always thought I just had really bad taste in men. I hadn't considered that I might have been part of the problem.

John sighed. "That's not important. Some of them were nice, just not right for you. One or two were on the down-low, if that makes you feel better."

"Not really. I thought my gaydar was on point." I sighed.

John went back to studying his star guide without saying anything.

"What if Gabriel is into me because I'm the only option he has?" I asked quietly.

John put down his star wheel and gave me a look that managed to be withering and full of love at the same time. "Fishing for compliments is gauche. Besides, Gabriel isn't like that. He's not very good at faking emotions, if you didn't notice during your first few interactions with him. He only plays nice when he means it."

"You really don't mind if Gabriel and I..." *become post-apocalyptic fuck buddies?* "...see each other?"

"As long as you spare me the details," John said, wrinkling his nose. "It's bad enough that today I found out that my parents are still getting it on." He shuddered dramatically.

An image of my parents flashed in my head. Not doing it—thankfully, I'd never walked in on that—but dancing across the living room to Motown oldies, looking into each other's eyes and laughing. They always laughed together. I tried to hold on to that image of them, that good memory, to avoid wandering down the mental path that was peppered with questions about their current well-being.

No matter what was going on, it was nice to think that my parents, in Cali, and John's parents, wherever they'd disappeared to, were making each other happy.

"I hope our parents are all getting it on somewhere right now," I said, letting the sudden drowsiness I felt envelop me as I drifted into a nap.

"Together?" John's voice drifted over. "What is wrong with you, Arden?"

I smiled and slipped into a deep, dreamless sleep.

13

My nap came to an abrupt halt when Maggie burst into the room.

"Time to get dressed!" she said. She flung something silky and black into my face and tossed John a tweed jacket to wear over his T-shirt.

I groggily pulled the material from over my head and blinked at it. It was black with little pink flowers scattered across it. "So John gets a cool professor jacket, and I get a bathrobe. Okay, then," I muttered, rubbing sleep from my eyes.

"It's not a bathrobe, it's a kimono, and a really nice one at that," she said, vibrating with nervous energy. She'd spent the whole afternoon preparing for the party, and her excitement showed. "PS, Arden, it's not like I could run out to the mall."

I shrugged and rolled out of bed, holding the silk robe out in front of me. It bore the scent of mothballs, but it really was beautiful. The hem pooled around my feet, meaning it would have been midankle on a non-Lilliputian person. I realized I was really going to have to learn how to sew if things didn't get back to normal.

"I thought kimonos were Japanese," I said, plucking at the wide sleeves.

"They are, but people give my parents all kinds of *Asian* things because they assume we're all the same. We also have some Chinese-style dresses and a random karate uniform."

I was tempted to take the karate uniform and stopped when I thought of Gabriel's warm gaze raking over my body. My bruises had finally faded and I'd been beaten my hair into some semblance of order, but it would be good to feel more than presentable. *Sexy. Desirable.* I'd spent enough time fantasizing about Gabriel's strong hands and soft lips, and it was nice to imagine knocking his socks off for once.

"I love it," I said, dropping the kimono on the bed and pulling my T-shirt up over my head.

"I'm going to go get ready," Maggie said, hurrying out of the room.

"I'm going to go...somewhere where I'm safe from half-naked black girls thrusting their asses in my face," John said playfully from behind me as I bent over to pull off my jeans.

"Nowhere is safe!" I called after him as he strutted

out of the room, rocking his tweed jacket as if we were at Fashion Week instead of in Bumblefuck during the zombiepocalypse, or whatever was going on outside.

I slid the kimono on and the silk felt wonderful against my skin, richer than I was used to and somehow sensuous. I secured the belt around my waist and stepped up to the mirror, where I undid my braids and fluffed my hair so that it surrounded my face in a kinky halo. My mane was a sad replica of its former glory, but it would do for the night. I swiped on the pink-tinted lip gloss Maggie had given me earlier in the week so I'd stop complaining about ChapStick withdrawal. The color worked well with my dark skin, giving my lips a natural-looking shimmer.

I gazed at myself with satisfaction, having fun with what used to be part of my normal weekend ritual. I ran my hands over the kimono, gathering the excess material in my hand and moving my hips as I spun around to imagined music. If things were normal, I would be getting ready for a night of dancing with my friends. As I moved to the music in the club, I would look across the room and see a pair of golden eyes staring at me, following my every move...

I noticed motion in my peripheral vision. Gabriel stood in the doorway, leaning against the frame in that insouciant way that had grabbed my attention during our first encounter in this room. His gaze wasn't weighed down with feigned laziness this time though. It was hungry. Ravenous, even. It seemed to me as though much too long had passed since we last touched each other, and the feeling was apparently mutual.

I made a yip of surprise as I stopped in my tracks, probably the least sexy thing I could have done in that moment, but his gaze only burned into me more. He took a step toward me, and I finally tore my gaze away from his and noticed what he was wearing. He always looked well put together, even in sweats, but Gabriel dressed up just wasn't fair. He'd used product to tame his shaggy waves, which curled perfectly around his ears. One button of his crisp black shirt had been left undone, revealing the creamy skin at the hollow of his neck and a bit of his smooth chest. I wanted to place my lips there, to feel his heartbeat against my lips. Not wanted—needed.

He reached me in two large strides, his dark denim jeans just snug enough to hint at the lean musculature of his legs as he walked.

"Is that what you'll sound like?" he asked in a low, urgent tone. He was so close to me, too close, and I had to tilt my head back to see his face. A wicked grin graced lips that were pink as a berry and, I already knew well, soft as silk.

"Huh?" I replied, unable to focus on his words with him crowding out everything in his proximity, including my common sense. I had wanted him to see me, to notice me, but I hadn't prepared beyond that.

"Is that what you'll sound like when you're under me, or over me, or however you'll have me?" he asked, sliding one hand up my back and resting it against my neck to ease the strain of looking up at him. The scent of something subtle but masculine wafted from him. Cologne? It wasn't aftershave. There was the faintest shadow of stubble on his chin, short prickly hairs that could scrape across my neck, my breast, my inner thighs...each part of my body throbbed as I imagined him teasing me with the friction. A sweet ache bloomed between my legs that could only be soothed by his touch. His calloused fingers slid into the hair at the nape of my neck, exerting just enough pressure to direct my gaze up. I wanted to feel his rough touch lower on my person, but even his fingers in my hair had me biting my lip against a moan.

He leaned down a bit closer, his deep voice triggering a shiver. It was like a low note on a guitar, one that resonated within you long after the higher notes had faded.

"Every time I've touched you, you've sounded different. I've been staying up nights wondering what you'll sound like when I really get you close to the edge. Will you cry out loudly, so I have to cover your mouth with mine to quiet you? Or will you make sweet little noises, like that one?"

By the time he was done talking, my head had lolled back, completely held up by his hand, and his lips were just inches from my own. Heat flooded my body at the thought of what he would do to find out the answer to his questions. Knowing Gabriel's perfectionist streak, and having felt his hands on my skin and his lips against mine, I had no doubt that he was fully capable of pulling sounds I hadn't thought in my vocal range from me.

But still, I couldn't let him know that all it took was a few words to leave me so needy that I was ready to blow off game night for the promise of what his lips and hands and other important appendages could do.

"You're feeling cocky, Dr. Seong," I said, lifting my head from his hand and taking a step back. "Who says you can get anything out of me?"

His eyes narrowed at the challenge, and his other hand slid into the opening in my kimono. It traced an excruciatingly slow path up my inner thigh, the drag of his fingertips leaving a sparking trail of heat in its wake. The closer he got to my juncture, the slower he moved. I had always categorized my legs as stubby, but the torment dragged on as if I had gams for miles. His face was still close to mine, gaze locked on me while he taunted me with those magic fingers. My nipples were taut against the material of the kimono and my knees actually shook in anticipation as his hand moved ever upward. My breath caught in my throat when he reached my apex, finally, and cupped me. I couldn't hide my shallow breaths, or the fact that I was damp with desire for him.

He smiled that lazy smile.

"Seems like I've gotten something out of you already," he whispered, his fingers giving me the lightest of strokes over my underwear. Something hot and desperate throbbed in my belly.

"Arrogant bastard," I whispered back. We were so close that my lips brushed against his as I spoke.

The bathroom door slammed from down the hall, and

we jumped away from each other, the brush of his hand as he pulled it away sending a pulse of need coursing through me. I hastily straightened my robe, and he turned to examine a book lying on the bed, hiding his evident excitement.

"Come on, guys!" Maggie hurried past the door in a hot pink tutu topped with a tied-off black T-shirt. Black high-heeled booties and a green dealer's visor completed the look. "The casino in purgatory is officially open for business!"

"I'll see you downstairs," Gabriel said. He retraced his steps, walking backward out of the room like he wasn't quite ready to look away from me.

I took a shuddering breath. I'd wanted to make Gabriel squirm, but he'd still managed to gain the upper hand. This called for extreme measures. I shimmied out of my underwear before retying my kimono and hurrying out of the room.

14

Maggie had prepared a delicious ziti for dinner using a cast-iron Dutch oven she'd found in the cellar. The unholy union of carbohydrates, melted cheese baked in the hearth and lycopenes combined to form the perfect comfort food, and we all ate with gusto, not worrying about rations or leftovers for once.

"Eat, drink and be merry," John said, candlelight reflecting in the glass of red wine he raised. We all returned his salute, even Maggie. Gabriel's attempt to stop her from drinking a small amount had been overruled.

"For tomorrow we may die!" she finished with giddy emphasis, sending a pointed look at Gabriel before taking a gulp. "Ugh! This tastes like dirty sock juice." She made a disgusted face, but then took another large sip.

"Easy there, Mags," I said. "You only get one glass, and then it's grape juice for you."

I glanced at Gabriel. I could see that he wasn't pleased about her drinking, but he was trying very hard not to ruin Maggie's night.

"It's an acquired taste," he said with a smile in her direction, sending her a wink. Her responding smile was radiant, and I was struck again by how much his opinion meant to her, despite her griping. The relationship between siblings was a mystery to me, but I was glad that Gabriel was suppressing his natural inclinations so that his sister could have fun.

I didn't realize that I was staring at him with a goofy smile on my face until he glanced in my direction and winked at me too. My cheeks burned, and I placed my glass on the table. The wine was delicious and fruity, but perhaps it would be wise to take my own advice.

Maggie stood abruptly, flashing a wad of multihued Monopoly cash, drawing all of our attention to her. "Are you ready to lose your money to the best dealer in town?" she asked brightly. She was so eager for us to have a good time, her occasional teenage sullenness replaced by a near-manic desire to please. I thought of all the fun nights I'd had with my friends since my teenage years, all the things she might not experience if life didn't return to normal, and found myself blinking away a random surge of tears. This night was more important than I'd realized, and I was going to do my best to make sure it went well.

"You have to teach me to play before you fleece me," I said, rising and linking arms with her as we headed toward the living room. I drew in a breath as we entered. "Oh, this is wonderful."

While we'd been lounging around, Maggie had been busy. The sofas had been dragged to one side of the room, facing a makeshift stage. She'd hung curtains on the wall to create the stage, and her guitar leaned against the wall, waiting to be played. In the space left empty by the rearranged furniture, she'd set up a poker table using a foldable banquet. Stacks of chips and decks of cards were organized neatly at the dealer's station, where she headed after wriggling free from my hold.

She sat down in her seat and looked at us expectantly, so we took our seats in front of her, making happy observations between sips of wine about what a great job she had done.

"This is amazing, sis," Gabriel's voice rumbled from the seat next to me. "I can't believe what you managed in such a short amount of time. Way to go!"

He reached over and playfully knocked her visor askew. She tried to feign annoyance, but her cheeks were flushed with pride, and from the wine, as she set the visor aright.

"Okay folks, here are the rules..." she said, suddenly all business. "Jacks or better to start, joker's wild, no funny business."

The next couple of hours passed with an abundance of laughter interspersed with tense standoffs between the siblings as they battled over Monopoly money. I didn't know how to play, and although they all tried to help me at various points, my progress wasn't so quick as to pose any real competition for them. I was down to my last few chips, chewing my lip in frustration as I decided whether to fold or go all-in. The fact that Gabriel sat next to me, legs spread wide so that his thigh and knee pressed into mine, was not helping. The rub of denim against silk was like the meeting of flint to stone. Each contact caused sparks of sensation to cascade through my body, and in each exquisite spark was the threat of dangerous heat that could blaze out of control.

Maggie raised her eyebrows at me, waiting to hear my decision. John sighed loudly and grumbled about amateur hour. Gabriel's gaze was trained on the cards he cupped in one hand. His other hand was under the table, where his fingers began to trace lazy circles on the exposed skin of my knee. I jumped as the sensation from his touch spread from my knee up the sensitive skin of my thigh and coiled in a delicious throb between my legs.

"All-in," I said, trying to sound normal as I pushed my chips in to everyone's relief. I glared at Gabriel and moved my knee away from his questing fingers before John or

Maggie noticed.

"Wise decision," he said, placing his cards facedown on the table and pushing his huge stack of chips next to my puny one. "Too bad you're going to lose."

He unbuttoned the cuffs of his shirt as he spoke and rolled the sleeves up, exposing the smooth skin of his wrists and forearms. I'd never noticed how incredibly sexy a man's wrists could be until that moment. My tongue darted out to moisten my lips as I imagined licking him there, from his palm to his elbow.

My nipples tightened at the thought, and I squirmed in my chair. When I chanced a look at Gabriel, he was looking down at me with that hungry look again.

"Show what you got, people," Maggie said impatiently. I flipped my cards over to appease her and reminded myself that this was her night. Whatever was going to happen between Gabriel and me would require a more private setting, anyway.

"Full house," I said, hoping I had the terminology right. "So...I win?"

Gabriel flipped his cards over, revealing a measly two pair.

"You were bluffing!" I laughed, grabbing at the chips that were now mine.

"I felt sorry for you," he said, with a shrug. "Or maybe I just wanted to see you smile. You're probably the first person I've met who hates losing more than I do. You've been scowling for an hour straight."

"I've seen Arden cheat at a game of Candy Land. Against a five-year-old," John volunteered, refilling everyone's glasses with the last dregs of the red wine. Maggie frowned when he skipped over her glass. "What's next on the agenda?" he asked her.

"A concert," she said, sounding a bit nervous.

I squeezed her hand. "You're gonna be great."

She nodded, but something in the way she carefully hid her face behind her bangs seemed off. She didn't meet my eyes before she excused herself to go to the bathroom for the third time since we'd started playing, but I chalked it up to teen moodiness combined with the wine. And she probably missed her folks. I certainly missed mine.

I followed John and Gabriel to the stage area Maggie had set up. John took the La-Z-Boy, and Gabriel glanced at me.

"I have good memories of that chair," he said in a low voice, and I flushed thinking of the massage he had given me there. We sat on the remaining love seat. I tried to leave room for the Holy Ghost between us, but Gabriel threw his arm along the back of the couch. His hand smoothed over my hair and settled across the pillow at my back, his long fingers resting on my shoulder. I knew he'd had only a small amount of wine, primarily because John was hogging the bottle, so this open affection wasn't alcohol-fueled. I allowed myself to revel in the thrill of that for a moment.

"'Freebird!'" John shouted in his imitation of a hippie, and I reached for one of the tea candles and waved it in the air.

"'Stairway to Heaven!'" I shouted back.

Gabriel just looked between us and shook his head, but he settled his arm behind me more comfortably.

Maggie came rushing back into the room, visor-free and visibly less nervous about playing. She slung the guitar strap over her shoulder and struggled a bit to free her long hair, her movements a little ungainly, before she struck a rock star pose amid our hoots and applause. Her eyes were glossy and a bit unfocused as she tuned the guitar.

Unease stirred in my stomach. Maybe Gabriel had been right about the wine. She'd only had a little though, hadn't she?

"This first song is for Mom and Dad," she said, and I pushed my worried thoughts aside. "There was a Beatles album they would play all the time at the store while they worked, and sometimes when this song came on they would do a silly dance we'd made up, called the Octotwist."

She launched into a serviceable rendition of "Octopus's Garden", which should have been jaunty and fun but had a melancholy air to it, the way she sang it. Her voice was low and smoky over the not-quite-perfect notes of the guitar, creating an original and haunting sound. I couldn't help but feel a selfish twinge of pride. Our hours of practice had really paid off.

The room vibrated with suppressed emotion brought up by this ode to their parents, and again I found tears pressing at my eyelids. Maggie's face was carefully hidden by her bangs, but when she played the last note she flipped them away to reveal red-rimmed eyes and a tight smile.

John, Gabriel and I broke out into a raucous applause, although no one asked her to play the song again. It would have been too much for our hearts. Luckily for us, she launched into lighter fare: a Coldplay cover followed by a Nirvana cover that showed the *Unplugged* album still held sway over teens everywhere.

"And my final song tonight will be 'I'm Sticking with You' from a band called The Velvet Underground. I don't know anything about them, because I don't have access to Wikipedia, but Arden taught me this song and I think it's cute."

Her voice rang out high and singsongy, just like we'd practiced, and my fingers followed along on air guitar as if I could will her to play the right notes. The song was short and sweet, and she played it perfectly. When she took her bow, I jumped up and hugged her, feeling like a proud stage mom.

"That was freaking awesome, Maggie!" I said with a smile matched in brilliance only by the one I received from her in return. Her cheerful side resurfaced for a moment, lured out by our ovation.

"Really?" she asked. "You don't have to say that just to be nice."

"Do you think I'd lie to you?" I asked in jest, but she looked at me for too long before replying with an unconvincing, "I guess not."

Something wasn't right. I wasn't a paranoid person, but Maggie was acting strange. I chalked it up to the fact that she'd spent the entire day in a manic state trying to make everything perfect for us and was probably crashing. I hoped that was the reason for her subtly erratic behavior.

"Now you play something, Arden," John called out, pointing at me with his empty glass. "Play that song I like."

"Maybe tomorrow." I stepped away from the makeshift stage. This was Maggie's moment. "Is there any baked ziti left?"

"I want to hear you play," Gabriel's deep voice rang out from the couch. "I'm the only one who hasn't caught a performance yet."

That edge of command in his tone that had initially driven me crazy now made me want to jump into his lap, but even that wasn't enough to change my mind.

"No, guys. Let's play another card game," I said. "Bridge, maybe? Pinochle?"

"Come now, Arden," John said. He had pulled out his Roman orator impersonation, which meant he really was drunk. "We demand entertainment!"

Maggie moved away from me, pulling the guitar strap over her head and thrusting it at me. "Here," she said, all laughter gone from her voice.

"I don't think I'm up to it tonight..." I began, my feelings in a whirl. I didn't want to steal Maggie's thunder, but I didn't want to make such a big deal out of not playing that she felt condescended to. "Why don't we do a duet?" I asked, placing my hand gently on her shoulder.

"If they wanted a duet, they would have asked for one," she said tightly as she shrugged my hand off and went to sit on the sofa. She looked up at me with a petulant expression on her face and I sighed at the unfairness of it all.

"Well, go on," she said, and John and Gabriel nodded, completely unaware that a sixteen-year-old girl was having her thunder stolen at their bidding. My buzz had been completely killed by the strange vibe coming from Maggie, but at this point the longer I put off playing, the more she would resent me. Best to just get it over with.

"One song," I said. "A short one."

"The one I like!" John repeated his demand. "It's like a lullaby."

I began strumming the simple notes to "Sea of Love," high and then low, glad that he hadn't asked for something more complicated than the songs Maggie had played. The words came then, and I was caught up in the thrill of hitting the right note, of harmonizing with the guitar. As good as it felt to perform, I kept the vocal theatrics to a minimum.

I glanced out at my audience. John swayed along to the music, Maggie sat stiffly on the edge of the sofa and Gabriel stared at me so intensely that I nearly lost my place. It was a simple song, but I couldn't help but feel that Gabriel's gaze added an additional weight to my words. I looked away from him, staring at the floor as I sang, but it was too late. John had requested the song because it comforted him, but I was singing for Gabriel now, whether I wanted to or not. Worse, everyone else knew it too.

As the last note of the song vibrated in my throat, my gaze met his and I was consumed by the unhidden desire blazing in their amber depths. Something between us shifted and reformed as we stared, like paper folded into origami. There was lust in his eyes, that was for damn sure, but there was a tenderness underlying it that filled me with a simultaneous hope and fear I'd never experienced before. In that moment I wanted everything from him, and he looked as if he was prepared to give it to me.

Maggie stood and stomped out of the room, swaying on her heels. Her abrupt exit broke our reverie, making me realize that there had been no applause when my song ended, just a loaded silence.

"Should I go see what's wrong with her?" John asked boozily from his seat. "And maybe give you two a moment alone?" He didn't move though, simply took another sip of wine before realizing that his glass was still empty.

"I'll go," I said, hurrying up the stairs after her. I wasn't exactly thrilled to be walking willingly into teenage drama queen central, but perhaps the night still be could be salvaged. More selfishly, a powwow with Maggie would give me a moment to collect myself away from Gabriel's knowing gaze.

"Maggie?"

Her door was cracked open, but I knocked before pushing it open. Either she didn't hear me or she didn't care because I found her sitting on the edge of her bed with a small minibar bottle of vodka in her hand. She gulped it down, grimaced and threw it to the floor, like someone who'd learned how drunk people acted by watching old sitcoms.

Well. That explained a lot.

"Why don't you go back down to your boyfriend?" she said when she finally acknowledged my presence, her tone jeering. "It must be nice having a boyfriend who isn't dead."

She was a mean drunk. Awesome. I was used to Maggie being cool with me, if not showing outright adoration, and her angry words stung. I scrambled to find the right thing to say to her, the thing that would counteract her vodka-fueled anger. She had only mentioned Devon a few times, and though it was plain that she'd been smitten, I hadn't given much thought to how his loss on top of that of her parents would affect her. I obviously should have.

"No, I think I'll hang out with you for a bit," I said, closing the door behind me. "It sucks that you can't contact Devon, but there's no reason to think he's dead. We're still alive. Why wouldn't he be?"

"Because his family was poor and didn't have a stockpile of food sitting around like we do," she snapped before sniffling and sinking down onto her bed. "I just miss him so much. I feel so alone here, and I never felt alone when I could talk to him. Or my parents. I could talk to them about almost anything."

I'd dealt with many a drunk during my stint at the pub, and her abrupt switch from mad to maudlin was textbook. "You have your brothers," I reminded her.

"Whatever." Her vulnerability disappeared with a curl of her lip. "It's not like they'd want to spend time with me if this disaster hadn't happened. They probably wouldn't even care if I left now. Why would they when they've got Arden the magnificent?"

I heaved a breath, remembering why I usually steered clear of teenagers and drunks, who had similar anger management skills. I tried to think of what my mom would say in this situation. She was good at comforting people, and even a good-for-nothing daughter like me had learned something from her over the years. She would always manage to respect your feelings but also point out the bullshit in your argument.

"Come on, Maggie. You might be mad right now, but whether your brothers care about you isn't something that's up for debate, and you know it," I said as I carefully picked my way across her room. The room was messy, like any teenager's, and it wasn't until I stepped over a pile of clothes that I noticed it peeking out from under the bed. The smooth wood grain of a baseball bat. The familiar notches in the grip, the burn mark from an unfortunate incident at a barbecue.

My Louisville Slugger.

"Where did you get this?" I reached for it slowly, hoping it was some kind of hallucination and my fingers would pass right through it. Unfortunately, they closed around maple wood, solid and familiar.

She jumped up unsteadily. For a second, her face was blank with shock, but then her brows drew together in anger. "Ugh, of course you would find it. What are you going to do, rat on me to John and Gabriel?"

"No, I'm going to keep talking to you until we figure this out. And I'm going to ask again—where did you get this?" Dread writhed in my stomach. Any answer she gave was going to be the wrong one. "I left this behind when I came here. I left it in the clearing where we were attacked."

I was startled by the way her eyes narrowed at me. I knew she was drunk and upset, but it hurt how she looked at me as if I was a stranger, as if we hadn't shared hours of laughter and kinship.

"Those were my footprints by the bodies, okay? I heard you and Gabriel talking that night, when you told him not to go, and I couldn't stop thinking about it...that those guys might have attacked my parents too. I knew Gabriel wouldn't let me go, or do anything helpful *ever*, so I snuck out that night."

My stomach twisted viciously at the thought of her outside in the darkness alone, where men like Blue Hat and his friend were eager to hurt someone. Of her rummaging among corpses for clues that would lead her to her parents' whereabouts.

"Maggie, something awful could have happened to you," I said, my voice so thick with emotion that it barely eked out above a whisper.

"Something awful already happened to me. In case you missed it, the world is ending and my parents are gone," she said. Her words were a little slurred, but her tone was as sharp as a shard of ice. "You know, I planned this entire night to show Gabriel I could be responsible, but he didn't even notice because he was too busy looking at you. When I heard you tell Gabriel not to leave the other night, I thought you did it because you cared about us. But now I think you just wanted him here because you're selfish."

Selfish? My body tensed as if trying to ward off a physical blow. I reminded myself that she was just a drunk kid, but her words were too close to what I actually thought of myself. "Maggie, that's not true," I said, trying to modulate both my voice and my emotions as tears stung my eyes. Did she really feel this way about me? "I care about all of you—"

"No, you don't care about us," she said, her voice rising and her insults gaining momentum. She wasn't listening to a word I said. Her inhibitions were gone and she was reveling in her drunken fury, directing her anger at the most convenient target. I knew how delectable that feeling could be; I'd been a champion spleen-venter myself back in my boozehound days. "You didn't want him to go because you didn't want him to find anything. I bet you hope our parents don't come back. You hope they're dead because your parents are probably dead, and you want us to be just as miserable as you are!"

I gasped and grabbed my chest. There was an opening in even the most well-crafted armor, and she had just landed a direct hit on a vital organ. Her words unlocked the thoughts about my parents I'd been hiding from since I'd arrived here. That they were dead, and they'd died knowing what a terrible daughter I'd been to them.

Something about my reaction had a sobering effect on her. Her eyes opened wide and she began shaking her head, her imbiber's remorse already setting in. "No, no, I didn't mean that. Arden, I'm sorry, please..."

Her words of regret poured out quickly, as did the tears now wetting her reddened face. She stumbled toward me, seeking the comforting forgiveness of my touch, but I turned from her and ran.

My face felt too hot, and the pressure that welled up in my sinuses and throat made swallowing painful. The kimono swirled around my feet, threatening to trip me, but I made it down the stairs and through the kitchen to the back door. I wrenched it open and slammed it behind me before falling to my knees in the snow.

Only then, in the darkness of the winter night, did I let the tears come. Huge, hiccuping sobs racked my body. I had fought the emotions for so long, fought my fear for my parents and my anger with myself, and it all came gushing out now, leaving me empty.

Somewhere in the back of my mind, I'd allowed myself the comforting thought that even if my parents were gone, at least I had this new family unit, this new possibility at happiness. This time, I wouldn't let anyone down. But the truth hurt; I'd never be part of this family.

I was alone.

15

I didn't know how long I knelt there. Frigid gusts of wind whipped at my tear-streaked face. My skin was all goose-flesh, and shivers shook me so hard that my teeth chattered uncontrollably. My fingers and toes burned from the cold, and still I didn't return to the house. Instead, I sat and thought of my parents, as if the penance of my pain could somehow give them comfort wherever they were, alive or dead.

The door opened behind me, and I was framed in a rectangle of dim light before a long shadow stepped through and the door closed again.

Hurried footsteps crunched through the snow. I recognized them as Gabriel's. Apparently he was destined to come rushing to save me from problems of my own making.

"Arden, what the hell—" he bit out, and then his

warm hands were on me, pulling me up like a rag doll and cradling me against him.

"Please leave me alone, Gabriel," I said in a dull voice.

"Great idea. We definitely need a case of hypothermia, and maybe some frostbitten digits for me to amputate." His words were gruff, but laced with worry.

My arms remained stiffly at my sides, but he hugged me close to his heat, pulling the edges of his warm down jacket around me and zipping me inside with him.

"Put your arms and legs around me."

I obeyed numbly, and I was snugly ensconced in warmth. I was amazed at how much heat his body produced. It was like being wrapped around a furnace compared to the extreme cold I had just endured.

"Do you want to go back inside?" he asked.

I shook my head. He walked toward the door, but instead of going in he continued until my back was pressed against the side of the house. His hands slid under my ass, giving me extra support. He hugged me to him in silence as my shivering subsided and my tears stopped flowing.

"Do you want to tell me why you let a drunk sixteen-year-old having a tantrum drive you out into the snow?"

I rested my head on his shoulder, unable to meet his eyes. "I was supposed to go visit my parents at Thanksgiving," I said on a shaky exhale, finally letting it all out. I hadn't even revealed this to John. "But I told them I was busy with work and that I'd come at Christmas. I wasn't busy. Business was slow, even. When they started asking me when I was arriving for Christmas, I stalled again, saying I was swamped and I'd get there in January, when things died down.

"The last time I spoke to my mother was to tell her I actually couldn't make it, but that I'd be there in February, for sure. And I heard it. I heard the moment when it clicked for her that I'd been lying, when she realized I'd been avoiding coming out to visit her."

The memory of the soft, slightly startled "Oh" my mom had uttered bought a fresh sheen of tears to my eyes. I shuddered out a breath, disgusted with myself. Although I didn't deserve the comfort, Gabriel rubbed a hand up and down my lower back.

"Why didn't you want to see her? I thought she was sick," he said.

"She is," I whispered. "She is, and I couldn't take it. I couldn't deal with seeing her like that, and that's the last thing my parents learned about their child. That I'm an ungrateful coward."

His chest expanded against me as he heaved a sigh, and his warm breath rushed past my ear on the exhale. I wondered what he was thinking of me, this man so dedicated to the bonds of family. Would he still want me now, knowing how I'd let down my own flesh and blood?

"Not wanting to see your mother suffer doesn't make you a bad person, Arden. People do crazy things when they're scared, especially when they're faced with a situation they can't control. I could go on and on about what I've seen from patients and their families at the hospital. I'm sure your mother understood that you were scared, and I'm sure she'll tell you that when you see her again."

I shook my head. "My parents are old, and my mother is sick. I've been trying to tell myself they're okay, but chances are they're not. It's been so hard hearing you guys be so optimistic about your parents returning, and knowing that mine are probably—"

"Enough with the self-flagellation, Arden," Gabriel interrupted. "You don't *know* anything right now, so quit imagining the worst. You can't change that you didn't go visit them. Shit happens. Do you really think that could make them love you any less?"

He had hit on *exactly* what made me feel as if I was in free fall every time I thought of my parents—that innate and overwhelming fear of disappointing those I loved the most.

"Arden, should I love my parents less because they left us here and ended up getting detained somewhere? Because if they'd just stayed with us, we wouldn't be worried to death about them right now. I get angry, but I still care about them more than anything. I'm sure your parents feel the same way."

I sniffled in response and shook my head. I had held on to this pain for weeks now, and letting it go would be losing yet another connection to my parents.

"Look at me," he said, his voice urgent and low and impossible to disobey. "I completely understand your sadness and your regret, but this isn't you. This giving in to the darkness and wallowing in it—it is not you."

"You barely know me," I said, distracted from my self-pity by his indignation on my behalf.

"No, you don't get to pull that again," he said. "That may have been true a few days ago, but not anymore. I know that you're bossy and tough and smart. That you care about people so deeply, even if you try to hide it under a veneer of sarcasm. And if I can figure that out after a few days, I'm pretty sure your parents know how much you love them, even if they found your actions hurtful."

A profound relief washed through me as I finally let his words have their intended effect. I didn't feel entirely guilt-free, but I knew he was right.

"Thank you," I whispered, wiping my tears away. In addition to warming my body, Gabriel had warmed my soul, as well. My sadness receded to the background, and I realized something—in the midst of tragedy and uncertainty, I'd finally met a man who knew me, the real me, and didn't find me wanting. A man who cared about me even though I was stubborn, and who, for all his controlling ways, didn't try to change me. One who'd listened to my greatest fears and absolved me of them.

"I know I should wish you were in California with your parents, but I'm damned glad you're here," he said, and I again felt that fluttering sensation in my chest, this time chased by a pressure that wouldn't ease, pressing me forward until my lips met with his.

I leaned into the kiss, savoring the warmth of his mouth. He responded with slow brushes of his lips over mine. My body was pressed against his and his fingertips were inches away from my own personal promised land, but it was the brief brushing of lips, the barest of touches, that sent an erotic throb through me. This kiss wasn't like the others. It wasn't driven by fear or lust or a blind need to be touched. The desire that was building within me as our lips clung for longer and longer was much simpler—I wanted Gabriel's mouth, and only his mouth, on mine. This lust was pure, unsullied by the circumstances that had driven us together.

Finally, his tongue slicked over mine, and the warm tangle quickened my growing need for him. I tried to pull him even closer, though my movement was restricted by his jacket. It was keeping me warm, even if it was limiting my ability to maul him; however, Gabriel was shivering in spite of having both his goose down coat and me wrapped around him.

"Am I too heavy?" I asked.

"Don't insult my manliness," he said, hefting me closer to him and slashing his mouth down over mine. His tongue delved into my mouth, a blatantly possessive action that made my entire body prickle with want, but I was distracted by his trembling again.

"Are you cold then? You're shivering. We can go back inside."

"No." He looked at me then, his skin bathed in moonlight, his eyes molten bronze beneath his hooded gaze. "It's not the cold. It's you," he said, abashed. "It's because of you."

The fledgling sensations that had fluttered in my chest during my previous interactions with Gabriel burst into full life then, a phoenix born from the simple realization that I cared for this man and he cared for me.

"I want you to touch me again, Gabriel," I said, surprised at how husky my voice sounded in the still night air. "I want—"

My words were cut off by a gasp of delight as his hand slid up under my kimono and his fingers found the throbbing warmth between my legs.

"Tell me why you're not wearing underwear right now," he demanded, his voice rough. His fingers slid over my sensitive nub in maddeningly slow strokes. He wasn't gentle, but the pressure he exerted was just right. My back arched as I pressed down into the voluptuous sensation, but my motion was stopped by the damned jacket. The sensitive peaks of my breasts had brushed against his chest midarch, and I returned to that position, rocking slightly to maximize the glorious duet of pleasure. "I know you were wearing them before, so at some point you decided to take them off. Why?"

"Because when you touched me upstairs, I wished there had been nothing between us," I answered truthfully. My last words were cut off by a sharp cry—Gabriel pressed my clit harder and circled faster. I'd said the right thing apparently.

"Arden," he groaned. He nudged my head to the side with his own and then his teeth dragged down the length of my neck, grazing over my skin with just enough pressure to make me both fear the pain of a bite and anticipate it. The pinch of sharp enamel activated some feral part of my lizard brain, and thick shafts of passion surged through me in response. I arched against him again, every muscle in my body tightening and releasing in response to his ministrations.

"So you were planning on seducing me?" he asked against my neck before licking at the place he'd just bitten. The slick passage of his tongue over the sensitized areas initiated pleasurable aftershocks.

"No," I said. "But I thought about how good it would feel to have you inside me and I didn't want anything to delay it. I just was trying to be proactive."

Gabriel's surprised laugh burst into my mouth as he kissed me. His lips were cold but his tongue was hot as it caressed mine. He stopped circling my clit and slid two fingers into my warmth, the friction of their entry sharp and satisfying. I bucked against him, clutching at his shirt. The focus of my mind narrowed down to the sensation of fullness as his fingers curled inside me.

He repositioned his hand so that his thumb was over my sensitized bundle of nerves, circling it while he thrust his fingers in and out. His mouth ravished mine as he worked me with that expert hand of his, and I cried out sharply as the taut string of desire within me snapped, flooding my body with pulses of euphoria that made my toes cramp. My mind was wonderfully blank as the last vestiges of my climax clamped around his fingers. He slowly withdrew them, leaving me feeling empty despite my satisfaction.

"I think I need to warm you up a little more thoroughly," he said, securing his hold on me before walking us back inside. He unzipped his jacket and set me down on the floor. My legs were unsteady and I placed a hand against the wall for balance.

"What about Maggie?" I asked, remembering what had driven me out into the night to begin with.

"Maggie is okay except for the monster hangover she's going to have from mixing booze. We talked a bit, but she ran to go hug the toilet and I decided to let her sleep it off. We're going to have a serious conversation tomorrow morning." He prodded me up the stairs ahead of him.

So she hadn't told him about the bat, about sneaking out of the house.

"But there's something else you should know," I said. I turned around to face him. Since I was a couple of steps ahead, I was taller than him for once.

"Something else can wait," he said. "Everything else can wait."

"But it's important," I whispered. "Really."

"Trust me, nothing is as important as this right now," he whispered back, nudging my nose with his. That small, goofy gesture and the way it made me spark with happiness settled it. Nothing could be done with Maggie down for the count anyway, so the unpleasantness could be saved for the morning.

We were at his room then, and this time he didn't leave me wanting in the hallway. I climbed onto the bed while he lit a candle and placed it on the bedside table, illuminating the small room. It had been converted into a guest room in shades of tan and peach and bore no hint of his personality.

He stood beside the bed, looking down at me with that molten honey gaze of his. His hands moved down the front of his shirt, intent in each controlled twitch of his fingers. I moved to help him undo the buttons, but he shook his head. "Take off the kimono," he ordered. I would have complied if I could stop staring at him long enough to undress myself.

Although I'd never found the male striptease particularly erotic, Gabriel's deliberately slow unveiling was the hottest thing I'd ever witnessed. My temperature rose with each newly revealed swath of skin, and heat flared at my core when he finally eased out of his shirt. He was beautiful. Every cut of his abdominal muscles was highlighted by deep shadows, and the sinews and veins of his arms were pronounced in the flickering light. His small, dark nipples stood out against the pale expanse of his chest—there was only the faintest smattering of hair, and something about the smoothness of his well-defined pecs made me want to lick him there.

I swallowed, my throat suddenly dry. He stepped out of his jeans; his gray boxer-briefs were tented at the front, the outline of his arousal beckoning me. I reached for him but stopped when he shook his head.

"Arden." The censuring tone in his voice sent a thrill through me.

I knew what he wanted.

I kneeled on the bed and untied the kimono slowly, tugging out the belt and dropping it beside me before sliding the silk off my shoulders and letting it pool around me. He grabbed the material in his fist and pulled it away, the drag of silk over my skin a delicious tease that left ripples of bliss in its wake. The kimono hadn't hit the floor before his hands replaced it, coarse instead of silken against my shoulders, then my breasts, my hips, my ass. His palms traced the outline of my curves, his touch alternating between reverent and rough. It didn't matter how he touched me, just that he didn't stop. I didn't move, or at least I tried not to. I couldn't control my trembling, or the way my hips bucked when his hands smoothed over my inner thighs.

I leaned forward and kissed his neck, tonguing that sweet hollow I'd so desired to touch earlier. He tasted salty sweet, and addictive. The muscles in his chest tightened and jumped, and I kissed them, too, my tongue darting out to lap at a nipple. He hissed, and I did it again, circling each one before venturing down his flat stomach. I licked over the ridges of his abdominals, exploring every crevice. As I swirled my tongue over the thin trail of hair that led toward his jutting erection, the warmth between my legs thrummed at the promise of fullness to come.

Gabriel's hands gripped my shoulders. "You don't have to," he said, but the hunger in his eyes didn't match up with his words.

"Have to do this?" I asked, licking at the head of his cock through the fabric that constrained it. There was a wet mark on his boxers now, and it wasn't only from me. His eyes closed and he held on to me harder, as if he'd fall over backward if he let go.

"I take it back. Do whatever you want," he said hoarsely.

I swung my legs around the side of the bed so that my face was closer to his groin. My core pulsed with excitement, but I was trying to take this slow. I stroked my hand over the imprint of his shaft and placed my mouth loosely over his head, blowing warm air over it while I stroked him. I teased him, and myself, that way for what seemed like ages, before dragging down his underwear and taking him firmly in hand. I traced the rim of his head with my tongue and then lapped at it with long, flat strokes that let me savor the tangy taste of him.

"Oh, fuck, Arden." He thrust against my tongue, blindly seeking the warmth of my mouth, and I opened for him. He stilled as my lips slid up and down his shaft. My tongue swirled around his flanged tip. I was working him with steady strokes of my hand when he suddenly pulled himself away from me.

I sat back and frowned.

"Lay back, beautiful." He fumbled around in the drawer of the nightstand, and I did what he said, my legs dangling over the side of the bed.

The foil of the condom wrapper caught the light before he tore it with his teeth, and I tightened with anticipation as he rolled it down over his penis. I spread my legs, ready for his entry, but he had other ideas.

He fell to his knees between my legs and threw my thighs over his shoulders before licking into me. I bit back a cry of shocked pleasure as tingling bliss cascaded over me; it was too much, and not enough. His tongue whirled over my hypersensitive nub like a dervish, giving no leeway as he drove me toward the edge. I threaded my fingers in his hair and gripped the wavy strands, pushing him away when the sensation became too intense. His hands squeezed my thighs to hold me in place, but one reached up to pinch at a nipple, rolling the peak while his tongue continued its onslaught. His fingers at my breast and his mouth between my legs took me from slow burn to inferno within moments. Pleasure scorched through my veins.

"Gabe, now. Please, I need you now!"

I was so close, and I wanted to feel him inside me this time. Not his fingers or his tongue, but that thickness that had fueled my fantasies for days.

I tugged at his hair, hard, and he finally relented. I scrambled back on the bed as he stalked toward me on hands and knees, mouth wet and eyes nearly black with passion. Only a thin ring of amber outlined his dilated pupils. I backed up into the headboard and waited for him to come to me, but he stretched his body across the bed and leaned back on his elbows, his member springing proudly from the patch of fine black hair at his groin.

"Ride me, Arden," he commanded, and I moved toward him, eager to do just that.

"Lazy," I said softly, resting my hands on his chest as I slowly lowered myself onto him. We both gasped when he pushed into me, the slow friction of his entry the sweetest torture. He leaned up to tease my nipples with his tongue, and I clenched around him, squeezing him with my inner walls. I leaned forward to give him better access to my breasts, and that slight motion changed the angle of entry just enough that he hit a wonderfully sensitive spot deep inside me. I'd thought we'd go slow, but I swallowed a cry as he rocked up into me fast and hard. My nails dug into his arms as I met each stroke, my hips moving in a tight figure-eight motion. His eyes were closed, his mouth slack, his expression one of pure desire.

I let out a low wail of frustration; the sensations built and built but didn't crescendo.

His hands grabbed my waist, hard, holding me in place as he thrust up into me savagely, somehow knowing exactly what I needed to get off. My gaze locked on to his and the desire to give pleasure that I saw there made my heart lurch and pushed me right over the edge. My eyes slammed shut and my mouth opened wide when the dam finally burst. I came, shuddering as the powerful tide of sensation swept through me, pulsing from my core to my stomach to my breasts. I wanted to scream my bliss, but some innate politeness silenced me, or perhaps my vocal chords couldn't process this new category of sound Gabriel drew from me. My breaths came in great gasps while I gripped him inside me, feeling him get even harder before he bucked up under me, small pants ripped from his throat as his eyes squeezed shut and his mouth pulled into a taut grimace of pleasure.

I collapsed onto his chest, his heartbeat jackhammering beneath my ear. We were both overheated and sweaty, but he hugged me tightly and dropped gasping kisses into my hair before pulling me down onto the bed with him.

"You..." He paused to catch his breath.

"Rocked your world?" I finished for him, grinning as he laughed and rolled so that we lay on our sides, legs entangled.

He stroked his fingertips across my jaw, across the areas where my bruises had faded. His eyes had returned to their normal amber color, and they studied me now. I studied him, too, trying to piece together all the strange thoughts and feelings that were popping up like weeds in a garden.

"You're not allowed to leave this bed ever again," he said with a bemused grin. His eyes retained their seriousness though.

"Even for a bathroom break?" I asked.

He held me tightly and shook his head.

"Bedpan," he muttered. And then he was kissing me again, fiercely. Possessively. I held on tight and kissed him back, just as hard. Who knew what tomorrow would bring? For tonight, we were safe and he was mine.

I awoke to something warm and wet moving pleasantly over the sensitive hollow behind my ear. I smiled when I recognized it as Gabriel's tongue. I'd become quite familiar with it during the course of the night. The way it could be pliant and coaxing or rigid and conquering.

I couldn't count the number of times we'd touched and explored each other, frantically— like students cramming the night before a final exam—before falling asleep with our arms tightly clasped around one another. The flutter in my heart every time I looked into his eyes scared the shit out of me, but I could at least rest assured that I wasn't the only one who was holding on for dear life.

We had repositioned ourselves into a spooning position at some point during our slumber. Now his forearm rested on my side, holding me close to him as his fingers brushed over my breasts. His thickening erection bumped me from behind, and his hips moved in lazy thrusts against the seam of my ass. I generally mauled anyone who messed with my sleep, but this was a wake-up call I wouldn't refuse.

"G'morning," I whispered, reaching a hand behind me to cradle the back of his neck. I ran my nails over the fine hairs and sensitive skin there, and he growled into my ear. His hand slid from my breasts down between my legs, where I was already aching for his touch, even though I'd only been awake for a few seconds.

His fingers slipped between my folds, circling slowly, the lackadaisical motion somehow ensuring that he hit all the spots that were crying out for his attention. Sensation tingled through me to my toes, my nerve endings preparing themselves for the pleasure that was to come.

I gripped his neck harder and he paused, kissing along my jawline.

"Are you too sore?" he asked quietly. "I can stop."

I ground against his hand. "Stop and I'll kill you," I said, working my hips so that my ass brushed against his erection.

He laughed that deep, bass tone laugh of his as he pulled his hand away, leaving me wanting. "I knew you wouldn't be a morning person," he said, rolling away from me. "I have just the thing for that."

"So death threats aren't enough to keep you at your

job?" I glared over my shoulder. My mouth curved into a silencing smile when I realized he was sliding on a condom. He was a lithe silhouette in the scant light that peeked in through the blackout curtains, so I turned and moved my hands to his hard chest and muscular arms, trying to take in his form with as many senses as I could.

It still seemed so unreal that I was here, that we were together.

His heart beat under my hand as I traced his pectorals with my palms, a sudden and unpleasant reminder of his mortality. My mind replayed the scene with Blue Hat, how Gabriel had strode into the clearing like an avenging angel, heedless of the danger.

I nearly stopped breathing at the thought of what could have happened to him. It was a crushing sensation; I felt like a tin can in a compactor powered by my own fears, bombarded by worries that would leave dent after dent until I was pounded into something small and sad.

He's mine now. Mine to lose. It could happen so easily.

I knew I shouldn't let these thoughts invade our first morning together, and I fought against them, but not before he heard the hitch in my breath as I pulled away from him. He caught my wrists before I'd moved more than an inch.

"What's wrong?" he asked. "Are you still worried about your parents?"

"No. Well, yes. But now..." I considered lying, but

there was no need for that between us. He could bypass any walls I threw up anyway, which was part of why I feared losing him to begin with. "Now I'm worried about you too."

"You weren't before?" he joked. I felt like a fool, revealing my fears to him. I could just imagine John making fun of me if he ever knew. *Girl, you dickmatized.*

But it was more than that. I couldn't explain the heavy feeling in my chest at the thought of something happening to him, how that mingled with the heady happiness that came from just being so close to him. Instead, I leaned forward and kissed him, taking him by surprise with the ferocity of my ardor. His mouth opened on a groan, and I took advantage, suckling at his plump bottom lip before nipping at it a bit harder than I should have.

His grip on my wrists tightened as he raised my hands over my head and laid me back down, his body blanketing mine. One hand secured my wrists while his other caressed my face, my neck, my shoulders, each touch dispatching a flurry of tremors through me.

He let out a soft laugh. "Why are you worried about me, again?" he asked, his voice rough. "I'm the luckiest man in the world right now."

His mouth lowered toward me, his warm lips pressing softly against mine as he kissed his reassurance into me. His approach was the exact opposite of mine, tender where I'd been rough. His tongue prodded gently, and I opened for him, welcoming the controlled passion of his movements as he subdued me with licks and nips.

His knee worked its way between my thighs, spreading me. When his hand slid over my mound and cupped me, it was no surprise to him that I was wet and ready.

"I knew we'd be this good together," he said as he stroked me. All I could do was nod and try not to cry out into the morning quiet of the house. "Maybe that's why we fought so hard." He settled himself between my thighs. "Because once we stopped, there was nothing to hide how right we were for each other. Because there's no going back from this."

I felt his cock nudge at my opening, already tightening in exquisite anticipation. I rocked my hips up to meet him, craving the thickness of him, but his hand pressed down at my waist, holding me in place. His weight was a constant pressure on me, although he took care not to crush me, as was the grip of his hands on my wrists and waist. I was entirely in his care, and my body trembled with the pleasure of it.

When he felt my body shaking beneath him, he finally slid into me and I welcomed the slow, relentless stretch. His breathing was labored and his muscles shook from strain, but he didn't change the pace of his entry, despite my attempts to speed things up. I undulated against him, trying to claim more of him, to quicken the pace of the erotic throb that built in time with his maddeningly slow stroke, but in this position I was at his mercy. He was in control of both my pleasure and his. When he'd filled me to the hilt, he circled his hips on the withdrawal and repeated the motion. He did this again and again, each slow slide of his cock building upon the previous thrust but going slightly deeper, circling just a bit wider. After I let go of the frustration, there was only a delicious fullness and the pangs of pleasure as he found a spot I didn't know existed inside me, plumbed some hidden depth. Sharp, brilliant bliss shattered me at the culmination of each stroke now, and I trembled with anticipation in between.

"I've got you, Arden," he said, only the slightest strain in that voice that made my knees go weak. "I'm not going anywhere."

The pace of his thrusting sped up, stoking the heat within me, and I struggled to move against him despite my constraints. My fears melted as he made love to me with the same fervent attention he applied to all of the things he cared about most. Strands of his hair brushed at my cheeks as he kissed me, capturing the tears that traced a path there. The tears didn't fall from fear anymore, but from the pleasure that sluiced through my body in waves, assailing me from every front: the friction of his cock inside me, the pressure of his hand binding my wrists, the gentleness of the kiss we shared, the way my heart felt full to overflowing. It all combined within me, some raw alchemical mixture of sex and emotion I'd never allowed myself to experiment with before.

The reaction was explosive.

I cried out into his mouth, arching madly beneath him as the sensation took me, as it both broke me and made me whole. My legs went up around his waist and held him to me as my inner walls clenched around his cock, and then he was gone, too, my climax pulling him along after me. Our moans intermingled between our breaths. He released my wrists and grabbed my face in his hands, holding me steady for a tender kiss even as the last wild thrusts of his hips subsided.

We didn't move in the aftermath. His forehead rested against mine and we lay there simply breathing in and out. I didn't know about him, but something within me had been utterly decimated, the high wall that had always protected that yawning need inside me. I didn't know if this was a good thing or a bad thing, but there it was.

A tentative knock sounded at the door.

"Oh my God, do you think they heard us?" I whispered, heat flooding my already flushed face.

Gabriel smiled—I could feel it through the darkness. "We can say it was those noisy deer again." He kissed my nose before rolling off me. "What's up?" he asked as he stood and disposed of the condom.

John's muffled voice came through the door, the voice of someone dearly regretting all the wine he'd drowned himself in the night before. "I know this is highly unlikely, given certain, um, sounds that have been emanating from this general area, but Maggie isn't in there, is she?"

I bolted up in bed, immediately on full alert. I may have been confused about some things, but *this* I knew was no good. Gabriel stopped midstretch, a still and silent shadow at the foot of the bed.

"Because I can't find her anywhere, and I'm a little worried," John continued. I was sure that if I had X-ray vision, I'd see him scratching his nose in agitation on the other side of the door.

Fuck.

I jumped out of the bed and my foot landed in a silky pile of fabric. My kimono. I pulled it from the floor and tried to find the armholes, all the while reassuring myself that Maggie wouldn't have been stupid enough to leave the house again. Despite the fact that she was an overemotional teenager. Despite the fact that she'd done it before—a bit of information that only I was privy to.

I heard the slide of denim over skin as Gabriel got dressed too.

"One minute," he barked. His voice sounded how it had the first time I'd met him—clipped and closed-off. Taking charge, but also taking everything onto himself. I didn't know if there was actually anything to worry about, but if there was, we couldn't go back to the way things had been. I'd flayed myself for him, and now he'd have to do the same.

I walked over to him, felt for his hand in the darkness and grabbed it. I could feel the slight resistance, the tension that emanated from him.

"There's something I have to tell you," I said, bracing myself. Against what, I didn't know.

He sighed, the deep, tired sigh of a man who was berating himself for not doing enough. For not being able to control all the factors that affected our lives. "Arden, I have to—"

"You don't have to do anything but listen. Once you do that, we can figure this out." I squeezed his hand, hoping he got my message. It took a beat longer than I was hoping for, but he squeezed my hand too. "Maggie told me something last night," I began, but then John shifted restlessly on the other side of the door, loudly cleared his throat and knocked again.

"You can tell us at the same time," Gabriel said, pulling the door open.

"Sorry," John said awkwardly. His eyes darted back and forth between me and Gabriel and our clasped hands, and he smiled. But it was a weak smile, overshadowed by the worry etched into his face.

"Nothing to apologize for," Gabriel said, despite the fact that he was shirtless and we looked like two people who'd had crazy sex all night long.

John started heading toward the stairs. We followed him, and the scent of already-brewing coffee, to the kitchen.

"I need caffeine. And aspirin," John said, rubbing at his temple with one hand as he poured coffee for all of us with the other. "Getting trashed so soon after a head injury isn't the best of ideas."

"Where have you looked for her?" I asked. "When did you notice she was gone?"

"She slept in the room with me last night, clutching a puke bucket, of course," he said. "I woke up about ten minutes ago and she wasn't there. I thought maybe she'd gone back to her room, since it's already afternoon, but she wasn't in her room or the bathroom or down here, either."

Gabriel let my hand go and cupped both of his around his mouth. "Maggie!"

Both John and I flinched, but that was the only response he got besides a ringing silence. Panic bubbled in my chest, and I felt tears pressing at my eyes for the umpteenth time in twenty-four hours, which had to be some kind of record.

She wouldn't have. She couldn't have...

"Maggie was the one who was creeping around the bodies," I blurted out, not sure how to relay the information delicately and opting for the sledgehammer approach. "I found my Louisville Slugger in her room last night when she blew up at me, and she told me she'd gone and searched them."

John's hand jumped and coffee splashed onto the counter when his head whipped in my direction. He clearly regretted the action, his face scrunching in pain as he squeaked out an incredulous, "What?"

Gabriel was silent. He watched me from across the kitchen, his expression stony.

"I tried to tell you last night," I reminded him. Tension started to gather between my shoulder blades, spreading up to stiffen my neck.

His eyes narrowed, but then he gave a curt nod. "You did," he admitted, and I felt a fraction of my worries ease.

"I figured she could tell you herself in the morning. It seemed like something you both should have heard from her," I continued. Part of me felt guilty that I hadn't forced Gabriel to listen, but I was tired of that particular emotion. I couldn't have predicted her behavior any more than they could have, and they had the benefit of a lifetime of observation. "I don't know if she left again—it would be ridiculous for her to leave—but you should know she's done it before."

"And here I thought she was such a Goody Two-shoes," John said wanly before swallowing some aspirin with a gulp of coffee. "Turns out she's just another alcoholic teen runaway."

"Let's just calm down," Gabriel said. "Why don't we check the house again? Arden, you take upstairs. John, you do this floor. I'll search the cellar."

We fanned out, calling her name. The search took less than five minutes, since the house wasn't that big. We were left with an unavoidable fact; Maggie wasn't there with us.

The three of us met again in the kitchen. I forced my cooled coffee down my throat while Gabriel trudged outside to see if she was nearby.

"Why would she do this?" John asked. "Did she smoke crack last night, in addition to getting wasted?"

"I have no idea," I said, and I didn't. All I knew was that I was scared and, if she'd left of her own accord, betrayed. How could she do this to her brothers at a time like this? How could she do this to me?

I stood and rushed up the stairs, quickly rinsing off with cold water before slipping into thick tights and my jeans, along with a warm wool sweater. I rummaged through a hall closet for a coat, since mine had been ruined by Blue Hat's blood, and found a nice goose down one that had the bonus of balled-up gloves in one of the pockets.

As I passed Maggie's room I ducked in, hoping the scene we'd had last night wasn't our final interaction. Her bed was unmade—it was never made, but now it seemed like one of those details that might be the last thing I remembered about her, and I hated it. I straightened her pillows and draped her duvet neatly over the wrinkled sheets just in case, a painful lump in my throat all the while. I hoped the bed would be messy again by night's end. I couldn't deal with another loss, with another relationship ended against my wishes and without me having a chance to make things right.

I stomped down the stairs in my Doc Martens, clutching my slugger, to find John watching Gabriel pack a bag.

"Her bow is missing from its case," Gabriel said without looking up. "And some food is missing from the cellar. Not a lot, but a box of her favorite snack was ripped open..."

His words seemed to wrap around me, binding me with the reality of the situation. I was unable to move, barely able to breathe, as it set in; she really had left. The smiling, sulking girl had surprised all of us.

"Where would she go?" John asked.

"She had a boyfriend in Florida, but I don't imagine she'd try to trek that far," I said, trying to figure out what the hell Maggie had gotten herself into. I'd expected embarrassment or anger and avoidance today, but not fleeing-into-the-wilderness-during-a-possible-apocalypse-level avoidance.

"How do you know all of this stuff?" John asked with an incredulous shake of his head.

"She talked about him during our lessons sometimes," I answered. "But it didn't seem like anything important until she mentioned him during her drunken ragefest last night. She was more upset about your parents not being here than the boy. Where does the chick they went to help live?"

"Darlene lives a couple of towns over, in a more remote area," Gabriel said.

"More remote than this?" I asked.

"It's a good day and a half hike from here. I didn't chance it before, since Maggie would have been here alone, and then you two came along but you were injured..."

His mouth clamped shut as he seemed to remember just how we'd come to be hurt. Our attackers were dead, but who knew what other monsters lurked out there waiting for Maggie to fall into their clutches?

"Goddammit!" I bit out. I wanted to punch a wall, or scream, or do something crazy to get rid of the dread and restlessness that made my skin crawl. I turned to Gabriel. "We have to go. Maybe we can track her?"

"Since when can you track anything, Sacajawea?" John asked, raising an eyebrow. He leaned back against the kitchen counter, arms crossed over his chest. "Weren't you the one who got us lost in the woods, and now you think you're gonna go save the day?"

His icy words stopped me in my tracks.

"I'm sorry, I'm such an asshole," I said, shaking my head as I realized my blunder. His words were harsh, but it was pretty jerky of me to plan around him as though he was window dressing when it was his own sister who was missing, on top of his parents. I didn't know what else to do with my energy, so I rushed over and hugged him.

His crossed arms pressed into my chest. "You're right. You should go with Gabriel."

"No, I'm the asshole. You're just trying to help." He gave a contrite sigh and then wriggled his arms free to wrap them around me. "This just sucks and I hate it. I fucking hate it."

"Light's fading. Which of you is coming?" Gabriel asked, hefting the bag onto his back. He slipped the pistol into his coat's deep pocket, and terror coursed through me. I sincerely hoped he wouldn't have a reason to reach for his gun.

"Arden, you go," John said. His arms slid up to my shoulders and squeezed tight. "I can use the shotgun to protect the homestead, and I know these woods like the back of my hand if I need to make a quick getaway."

We agreed to rendezvous at a place familiar to the brothers if anything happened at the house.

"Have the gun and one of the go bags near you at all times. We'll try to check in if anything comes up, so keep your walkie-talkie on," Gabriel barked. He stalked over and stared down at his brother before pulling him into a rough hug. It wasn't lost on me that they were the last two account-ed-for members of a rapidly shrinking family. We had all lost so much in the past few weeks. I gripped the edge of the kitchen table tightly and closed my eyes. After taking a deep breath, I sent a wish to the universe that nothing more would be taken and that all would be restored. Like I'd said to

Maggie during our first foray into positive thinking, it didn't hurt to put it out there. We needed all the help we could get.

The sound of Gabriel's footsteps passed me, and I opened my eyes to see John holding up a walkie-talkie that looked as if it had been invented shortly after the telegraph.

"Do those things even work?" I asked doubtfully as Gabriel stuffed the matching walkie-talkie into an inner pocket and zipped his jacket. Both of them ignored me, and I chose to interpret that as "yes, they're fully functional."

John's eyes latched on to mine, fear broadcasting from their dark depths. "Take care of my brother," he said. He turned to Gabriel. "Take care of my Arden."

Gabriel nodded and opened the door to the freezing air and wintry whiteness beyond. I felt rooted in place. The house had become my refuge, and being forced from it was terrifying. But Gabriel started walking, and I took one hesitant step after him, and then another.

"Be safe," John said as he stood in the doorway watching after us.

"Make sure you have dinner waiting for us, darlin'," I said in a faux frontier-man voice, and he gave me exactly what I needed—that sunny smile of his. Then the door closed and the locks clicked.

"Ready?" Gabriel asked. His face was a blank slate, all of his anger and fear tamped down under his sense of duty. But he still reached out and pulled me close.

His lips pressed into mine quickly, leaving a lingering warmth behind. "Thanks for having my back," he said as he started forward, eyes now on the ground searching out Maggie's footsteps in the snow.

"Anytime," I murmured, walking close behind.

17

I had thought it frigid before, when John and I had trekked miles and miles in the snow to reach what we'd thought would be refuge. Now I knew that frigid was just a mile marker on the way to whatever temperature it was as Gabriel and I searched for Maggie. My eyeballs hurt from the cold, and the snow was covered with a treacherous icy crust that made for slow going even with our boots' reinforced soles. Occasionally, we'd get the awesome surprise of stepping onto a weak spot and plunging in up to the knee.

Funny, when we'd made that first trek, I'd only hoped for a place to stay that was safe and warm and had something to eat besides stale nuts. The thought that I would meet a man I was starting to fall for and a teenager who I'd be out of my mind with worry over had never occurred to me. But here I was, following said man and searching for said teenage friend—that was what she was, I realized. A friend. Despite our argument, despite the fact that I would throttle her when we found her, Maggie was no longer some hypothetical extension of John. She was flesh and blood to me now, and I knew all too well how easily she could be hurt.

"I am going to murder her," Gabriel said through clenched teeth as he kicked at some icy brush with the toe of his boot.

Not if someone else has done that already. I stomped forward, as if I could crush the pernicious thought underfoot.

"I'm just going to set her on fire," I said, an odd attempt at keeping things light.

Gabriel turned to look at me, the winter sunlight reflecting off the snow and illuminating those beautiful eyes of his.

"What? It's freezing out here and she's flammable. Inflammable. Whatever," I said with a shrug as I turned in a circle and surveyed the area, trying to remember what little I'd learned during my brief fixation with *Little House on the Prairie.* They'd had to search for one sibling or another in the snow, right?

*Tree, tree, tree...*the surroundings all blurred together, until my eyes alighted on a hot-pink beacon in the midst of the tree bark.

"Shit."

The word slipped out of my mouth, and Gabriel was

already following my line of sight, running toward the fuchsia-fletched arrow embedded in the tree trunk ahead of us.

He stopped short, almost skidding to a halt on the icy crust covering the snow. I jogged over to him, my stomach dropping at the sight before me. There was a deep indentation in the snow. If we'd been at the local park, I would have guessed that a couple of giant dogs had been rolling around having a grand old time, or perhaps that a very uncoordinated sumo wrestler had tried to make a snow angel. But we were in the middle of the woods, and Maggie was missing. What we were looking at was what they would call "signs of a struggle" on the police procedurals I used to glom.

The arrow stuck out from dead center of the tree. One set of footsteps approached it from head-on, small steps that dragged a bit, like most surly teenagers'.

A second set could be seen approaching from behind, but at an angle. These were widely spaced, and it didn't take an experienced tracker to figure out that this person was much larger and had been running. There was a disturbed area of snow where they'd struggled, a stomped-in and kicked-up circle where Maggie had fought her opponent.

She's tough, like you, Arden. She wouldn't go down without a fight. Maggie's words from dinner just a few nights ago rang in my head as Gabriel hunkered down and grasped at something in the snow. A long strand of black hair hung from his fingertips. Crystals of snow clung to it, sparkling like diamonds in the afternoon light.

There was a trail leading from the impromptu out-door fighting arena, a trail left by flailing legs that had dug deeply into the snow and kicked out at branches, seeking purchase. Or leaving a way for us to find her. Either way, I was impressed underneath the metric shit-ton of fear pumping through my system.

Gabriel was still hunkered down, staring at the strand of hair. I crouched down next to him, aware of the fact that we'd been in this position before, but last time, John had been bloodied before us. Hurt, but alive and accounted for.

The strand shook gently, and for a second I thought it was the wind, but then I saw the shattered expression of Gabriel's face and knew that it was him. Impotent fear crept over me on little icy feet. I was sitting right next to him, but I couldn't undo whatever had happened to Maggie. My heart was thudding in my chest and I was ready to rip the woods apart looking for her, but Gabriel was cocooned in his own personal horror story. I wrapped my arms around him awkwardly, holding him close and trying to transmit security and calmness that I didn't feel within.

"Let's go get her," I said quietly.

He glanced at me, the fear sharp in his eyes, and I shook my head in answer to the question he hadn't had to ask.

"No time to worry about what-ifs," I said, trying to infuse my voice with the command that came so easily to him.

He nodded and lurched to his feet, pulling me up with

him. His face was blank now, and deathly pale. I couldn't imagine how he felt; I'd only known her a short while, and the coffee I'd downed before leaving was surging at the back of my throat. This, combined with what had happened to his parents, and to John and—it seemed presumptive to think this, but I knew it to be true—to me, this had to be very near the straw that would break the camel's back for him.

"She's waiting on us," I urged, following the trail that led into the woods. He nodded again, and came after me. I was genuinely worried now. Gabriel's go-to self-defense method was withering remarks or general assholishness, and I was pretty sure that us having bone-shatteringly great sex hadn't magically changed that side of him. The fact that he was silent as we walked spoke to just how close to the edge he was.

I didn't think he'd want to be pitied, but I threw my hand back and held it there. His thick-gloved fingers closed over mine and we both hustled forward through the quiet trees. I fervently hoped that at the end of this trail wasn't a scene that would haunt us both forever.

My breath quickened as I thought of Blue Hat sitting on my chest, eager to hurt me just because he could. I didn't let my imagination stray to any similar scenarios involving Maggie. Any time a bad thought crept up on me, I bit my tongue, hoping the pain would serve as a sacrifice that would keep my horrid thoughts from coming true.

We were walking quickly, trying to remain quiet but opting for speed over the element of surprise. Quite suddenly, it seemed we wouldn't need it.

The silence of the crisp winter morning was broken, but not by us.

The wail scared the shit out of me, a banshee crying out from the depths of hell. But then there was a hiccup, a quieter cry and the familiar pattern that had ruined many a flight, movie and restaurant dinner in my time.

A baby. There was a goddamned baby at the end of this trail.

We ran then, thrashing through frozen underbrush and slipping on icy snow, fingers freezing as we dug them into the snow to maintain an upright position.

We were on them before we knew it.

Maggie kneeled in a patch of skinny young spruces, mouth gagged by a green bandanna and arms drawn up behind her like she was bound. Her red-rimmed eyes widened when she saw us approach, the tracks of frozen tears cracking on her cheeks as she began to yell.

There was a figure in front of her wearing a bulky white down jacket. Gabriel had slipped off his gloves while he ran, and the gun was in his hand now. He didn't pull the trigger quickly, as he had with Blue Hat. His hand was unsteady and his eyes were tight as he took aim. The figure spun around, and a ruddy, haggard face peered out from under the hood. A woman, not much older than me judging by her appearance, gaped at us. Her gaze swept over me, but landed on Gabriel and stuck.

"I told him not to do it," she sputtered. "I told him to just let them go, but he was coming off his fourth tour, and he was supposed to be taking his meds but he ran out. It's the PTSD, and he says chemical agents messed up his brain or something."

"Um, what are you talking about?" I asked, inching toward Maggie.

The woman didn't seem to be armed, but she suddenly lunged for the zipper of her coat, sliding it down and grabbing at both lapels.

I heard the safety click off on Gabriel's gun and wished this didn't have to happen. Again.

"Don't hurt the baby!" she cried, ripping the jacket open to reveal a red-faced infant strapped to her chest like adorable, snot-nosed C4.

"Fuck!" Gabriel yelled, quickly pointing the gun down and slipping the safety back into place.

The baby cried out, perhaps sensing something momentous had just happened.

"Don't hurt us," the woman who had to be Darlene cried out. "If you hurt us, I can't tell you where your parents are."

18

Gabriel had gone still, his eyes burning with hatred as he stared at Darlene, who stood dumbly petting her child like it was a lucky rabbit's foot that could keep her safe.

When Gabriel spoke, his voice was low and ugly, shocking me with its ferocity. "You kidnapped my parents and my sister, and you *dare* try to bargain with me?" he bit out. "Why should I give a fuck about you or your baby?"

Muffled sobs from behind Darlene caught my attention, and I hurried over to Maggie and pulled the gag from her mouth. I was frightened by the fury Gabriel was unleashing, but I trusted him. I'd seen the desolation in his eyes after he'd killed Blue Hat and friend, and I was positive he wouldn't hurt a woman who had a new baby to care for, no matter her misdeeds.

"I'm sorry, I'm so sorry!" Maggie sobbed. Her words came out in strangled squeaks. "I just wanted to get some air, I wasn't going to travel far, I swear. I was about to head home when he jumped me. I tried to fight back—"

I pulled her into a hug and she leaned into me, raising her arms up behind her. My fingers worked at the rope tied around her wrists as she sobbed into my jacket. When her hands were free, she threw her arms around me.

"Arden, I can't believe what an idiot I was last night," she said through a voice thick with tears. "I kept thinking I would die and the last thing you'd remember of me would be those hateful words. I didn't mean them, and I wish I could take them back."

I had thought my heart was already too full to bear, but I was wrong. I refused to let my tears fall, but I squeezed the annoying teenager who'd crept past my defenses and into my heart, and hoped my next words were true. "It's okay. We're gonna be okay," I said, my eyes on Gabriel and Darlene, who were staring at each other. The baby hiccuped and whined a bit before quieting down, and Darlene rubbed its little belly soothingly. It was so cold, and despite the idiocy of its parents, I was worried for the small thing.

You would think that dealing with an apocalypse would harden a person, but I was getting softer by the moment. If a woodland creature jumped out right then, I would have dissolved into tears.

"I couldn't stop him," Darlene finally said, forlorn. Tears began to stream down her face, and words from her mouth. "The baby came early and your parents stayed to help, but then Dale showed up out of the blue. What was I supposed to do? He's my husband. I love him. I promised to stick by him in sickness and health, and he's real sick.

"They'd shipped him back because he got into some trouble and needed R & R. I thought the episode would pass, and he'd let your parents go, but it didn't. It's not his fault he can't get his medication. I have no idea what the hell I'm doing with this baby or how we're supposed to survive. Dale told me he'd hurt us, too, that we were either with him or against him. I'm so sorry."

The woman was sniveling and shaking like a leaf, and I was shocked to feel a twinge of compassion for her too. I couldn't find it in me to despise her even if I hated what she'd done to survive.

Gabriel stared at her hard. I could sense him going over the horrible options in his head. His eyes widened and his mouth screwed up, and for a second I was sure he would shoot her out of frustration. Instead, he spat out a string of expletives as he walked toward me and Maggie, who was still sobbing. He enveloped the both of us in his arms, resting his head against Maggie's while briefly closing his eyes in relief. It felt good to be hugged like that.

It felt like home.

When he opened his eyes again there was less fury and more fear. "Where are my parents?" he asked.

"They're in their van, it's parked a mile or so away,"

Darlene said. "They're okay, just tied up. God, that's an awful thing to say, 'just tied up,' but I was so scared he was going to kill them this morning. They're alive and unhurt."

Relief washed through me, and I felt the tension in Gabriel loosen just a little bit. Maggie cried silently, as her relief had apparently struck her mute. But despite the fact that one mystery had been solved, there was another more pressing one.

"Where's your husband?" Gabriel and I asked at the same time.

"He's going to your parents' cabin," Darlene said in a small voice. "But you're all here, so no one will be hurt. That's good, right? Maybe together we can talk him down."

The baby made a disgruntled noise as she spoke, and she bounced him as if they were at the park and not in the midst of a hostage crisis. The whole situation was surreal, especially because her chipper wrap-up was wrong.

"Is John at the house?" Maggie whispered into my coat. Gabriel and I were already surging to our feet, which answered her question.

Gabriel pulled out the bright yellow walkie-talkie and tried to hail John, but his urgent attempts at communication were only returned with bursts of static. I hated being right sometimes.

"Do you have the keys for the van?" Gabriel asked, stuffing the walkie-talkie back into his interior pocket, and Darlene nodded eagerly, wanting to stay on his good side.

"Arden, pat her down and make sure she has no weapons."

"She's got nothing," I said after as thorough an examination as I could manage. I didn't think a cavity search was necessary, given the layers of clothing we all wore.

Gabriel turned to his sister. "Maggie, have Darlene take you back to the van and release Mom and Dad. Bring them to the house if you can. We're going to go make sure John is okay."

Maggie's eyes widened, or at least the one that wasn't hidden behind her long bangs. "You want me to go alone?" she asked in shock.

"I trust you, Mags, and I need you to do this right now." I knew it was taking a lot for Gabriel to send his little sister off into the wilderness with a strange woman. A few days ago he'd barely been able to let her cook for herself, but they both had grown in their parents' absence. He mussed her hair. "Mom and Dad need you."

She gave a quick nod of her head, seemingly fortified by her brother's words.

"Here, kiddo," I said, tapping her with the Louisville Slugger and handing it over. "I guess it was meant to be yours. Be careful, okay?"

"I will be," she said. "If I let someone get the drop on me twice in one day, I think my parents would disown me."

I didn't think it would be nice to point out that her

parents had been held captive for a week, so I simply gave her a smile. The corners of my mouth dropped when I turned to Darlene, who was waiting to lead her to the Seongs. She gave me a look that hinted at solidarity, as though we were on the same team, but I shook my head at her. "You even think about trying something funny with her, and that baby's gonna need a wet nurse. You understand?"

She nodded, and then they headed off in the opposite direction.

Gabriel heaved a sigh beside me, and I took his hand as we began to pick our way back through the icy snow, retracing our steps and hoping John could hold off Dale until we got there. I was actually hoping that a bear would intercept the guy midroute and eat him, thus saving us the trouble, but it was hibernation season, so our chances of assistance on that front were pretty slim.

"I'm doing a bang-up job here," Gabriel said as we jogged toward the house, frustration lacing his words. "I'm supposed to be protecting my family, and I've let everyone down. Right now, none of them are safe."

I made a frustrated sound in the back of my throat; it was a tic I'd picked up from my mom, having had it directed my way early and often.

"Let me break something down for you, sweetie. Safety is an illusion." He didn't look at me as we hurried over the snow, but I knew he listened as I spoke. "We thought we were safe in our apartments and in our SUVs. We thought our smartphones and our laptops meant we could cocoon ourselves away from the big bad world. But we're never safe, no matter how long the grace period. You can try to fight it with all your might, but unless you're some all-powerful being and forgot to tell us, you can't stop every bad thing from happening. You're doing your best, and everyone loves you for it. That's all you can ask of yourself."

As I said the words, I realized that maybe I should take a bit of my own advice. Beating myself up over not visiting my parents wasn't going to result in me sprouting wings and flying to Cali. Until I was able to get to them, all I could do was try my best to survive.

Gabriel still didn't look at me—his eyes were glued to our tracks as we jogged over the snow—but one corner of his mouth quirked up. "So, you're admitting that *you* love me for it?" he asked in that low timbre that did things to my insides that no human voice should be capable of.

My heart sped up and my mouth went dry. I really had walked right into that one. "You really are one cocky SOB."

"'Combative when asked simple questions.' Another addition to your patient profile," he said. He tugged me toward him for a quick kiss as we jogged. Our lips had just met, the sweet warmth a pleasant contrast to the cold, when we heard it.

A shotgun blast echoed through the silent woods.

We didn't even look at each other, just took off at a stumbling run, both of us knowing that whatever awaited us wouldn't be good.

19

"Shit. Shit, shit, shit!"

I muttered the expletive as I fell repeatedly in the icy snow, each time pushing myself up and trying to propel myself toward John. I would not see him hurt again. I refused. To hell with a bear; *I* would take Dale to pieces.

Gabriel was faring slightly better, but the ground was treacherously slick and he struggled to keep his balance too. The sky had clouded over, obscuring the sun and smothering the few warming rays that had been bestowed on us earlier in the day. The snow that had melted now refroze under our feet as we ran. I could taste the strange electrical flavor, like a battery on your tongue, that signaled a heavy snowfall was coming.

My lungs burned from exertion and I was really

regretting that I'd used the apocalypse as an excuse to slack off on my cardio, but we were finally drawing closer to the house.

"We're getting close," Gabriel huffed, slowing down his pace. We needed to be more cautious now. It was dawning on me how dangerous this situation was. This wasn't two hicks with a slingshot, but a trained soldier who'd just returned from combat and wasn't mentally stable. He might have already hurt John, and he might hurt Gabriel next. I could lose them both in one fell swoop. My legs stopped of their own accord, bound by invisible bands of fear. I knew I had to go forward, but I stood in place as waves of anxiety pushed at me from all directions. I would have stayed rooted to the spot if Gabriel hadn't turned and looked at me expectantly.

I had to watch his back. We had to get to John.

I scrambled behind him, trying not to think of what Darlene's husband might be capable of. There were two of us, hopefully three, and only one of him, after all.

The back of the house was coming into view behind the trees when we heard the sharp snap of splintering wood. Dale stood at the back door, jumping lightly on his toes as if he was warming up before a game. He wore a black-and-gray camouflage jacket with matching camo pants, and it was clear the pattern wasn't a stylish affectation. He gripped his hunting rifle in both hands before rearing back and kicking at the door with all his might. He wasn't a large man, but there was a wiry strength to him and a rabid determination behind each blow as he kicked and kicked.

"Get the hell out of here!" John's voice filtered through the door. "I don't want to hurt you but I will."

"And I don't want to hurt your parents, but if you don't open this door I'll blow them away, you greedy bastard," Dale roared. His voice was furious, as though he had some personal vendetta against John. "Keeping all the food for yourself while folks are starving. I served my country. I deserve that food!"

As we got closer, I could see that the door was starting to give, opening a bit with each blow before being slammed shut. My stomach dropped as I realized what the physics of that meant. John was on the other side, pushing against the door with his fine-boned body. He wasn't weak, not by a long shot, but he couldn't hold out against this onslaught for much longer, while Dale seemed like a kicking machine with infinite energy stores.

"Just go away, you psycho!" John yelled. I could hear frustration and disbelief under his fear. "All you had to do was ask, and I would have helped you."

"Liar!" Dale roared. He was breathing heavily now, but still trying to get through the back door with single-minded focus. He didn't hear us coming up behind him.

Gabriel was ahead of me, handgun drawn and almost close enough to pounce, when Dale finally stopped kicking.

"I gave you a chance," he said, pumping his rifle and

blowing a hole through the door.

"No! John, no!" I realized the horrific yelps were coming from my own mouth, being torn from my throat by anguish. There was silence on the other side of the door, but Gabriel was throwing himself at Dale with a roar.

"Motherfucker!" he growled, coming down with an elbow in Dale's back.

Dale grunted in surprise and stumbled forward, dropping his gun, which skidded across the icy ground. He didn't fall though. He caught himself midfall, braced himself on his hands and kicked out behind him, catching Gabriel in the stomach and turning the momentum of his furious charge against him.

Gabriel fell to the floor and clutched his sternum, his face contorted in agony. Dale was already on his feet, taking two hopping steps toward Gabriel before kicking him in the side with the form of a seasoned footballer. Gabriel cried out, writhing on the ground. His hands flexed in instinctive reaction to the pain, and his gun fell to the ground.

I watched the scene unfold with a strange sense of dissociation, even as my body was moving to join the fight. This wasn't how it was supposed to play out, not with Gabriel's strength and smarts. Everything had gone pear-shaped in a matter of seconds and my brain wasn't processing this alternate outcome quickly enough. Only when Dale kneeled and snatched up Gabriel's gun did my neurons start firing again.

"Another one of you greedy gooks," he sneered,

palming the gun. "My grandfather killed lots of you when he served, so I guess I'm just carrying out a family tradition."

Dale geared up to unleash another kick. I ran from behind him and jumped onto his back before he could let it fly. I was acting on instinct, thinking of nothing but stopping the man with a gun from hurting Gabriel. I realized it was the wrong move as soon as I was on him. His jacket was slippery and my legs flailed as I tried to gain purchase. I struggled to get a forearm around his neck, both to maintain my position and to choke him out, but he pried my arms open and flung me away from him with an ease that was frightening. I was small, but not that small. I'd heard that people who weren't lucid could have superhuman strength, but nothing could prepare you for being on the receiving end of it.

It seemed to take forever, my flight across the yard, but it had been seconds at most. I hit the icy snow hard, my teeth rattling in my head from the impact. I bounced and rolled a couple of times, a sharp chunk of solid snow cutting into my cheek as I skidded to a halt. The stinging pain and the warmth welling down the side of my face shocked me into awareness.

I opened my eyes and saw something nestled in the small-scale range of ice-capped mountains that had formed in the snow. Dale's rifle. I looked over my shoulder at Gabriel, who'd scrambled back in some semblance of a crabwalk and was now a few feet away from Dale. The guy had already marked me as down for the count and now ignored me.

"It's over, man," Gabriel said in his soothing voice.

"You hear that? It's your wife, and my sister, and my parents. And your baby. You've got nothing to win by shooting me. Just be cool and we can figure this out."

Only after he said it did I hear the sound of tires over hard ice, of snow crackling beneath treads.

"Just put the gun down and let me go see if my brother is okay," Gabriel said, rising to his feet as he spoke. He kept his hands in the air to show he meant no harm. I wondered if he could see me in the distance, picking up the rifle and heading toward him and the madman.

I wished John would make a noise or a groan or something. This silence was killing me. Knowing that Maggie and their parents were approaching and Dale still had a gun was killing me. I wished I didn't have this rifle in my hands, this weapon that opened up an entirely new world of responsibility and decision-making.

"No," Dale said, recalcitrant. "I came here to get supplies for my family and I'm not leaving without them."

Anger flared in me at Dale's sense of entitlement. Telling a man to his face that he was going to take what was his. Blue Hat looming above me and the sensation of his body on mine were suddenly as real as Gabriel and Dale. The memory faded, but my hands shook now as I raised the gun and took aim at Dale, trying to recall what Gabriel had taught me. Center mass. Remember the kickback.

"I'm not going to let my brother bleed out. You can have supplies if you want, and no one has to die for it,"

Gabriel said. His brow was drawn in frustration, but his tone was calm. There was still a trace of command there, though, even if he wasn't the one with the gun. He was edging around Dale, making for the back door, and for a second I thought it could work out okay. But Dale began shaking his head furiously.

"I didn't come here to beg from some gooks," Dale said through clenched teeth. "I don't need no charity, and I don't need your permission."

"Wait—" Gabriel didn't have a chance to finish his sentence. Dale squeezed his finger on the trigger. There was a loud blast, and then Gabriel was clutching his chest and falling backward. It didn't happen in slow motion, like in the movies. One minute he was standing, the next he was on the ground. Shot.

Pain of a different kind ricocheted in my chest as I watched him go down, the beautiful man who'd saved my life and my heart.

This isn't what's supposed to happen.

The rifle jumped in my hands and the stock whacked into my shoulder hard, knocking me to the ground. My ears rang from the blast—I had pulled the trigger without thinking, a macabre reflexive reaction in response to Dale's unfathomable behavior.

Dale's back looked different now, dark, pulpy fluid staining his camouflage jacket and blood splattering the snow around him before he crumpled into a heap. Darkness ebbed at the edges of my vision as a faint threatened to pull me under, but I fought the disorientation and scrambled over to Gabriel. His chest was heaving and he pulled fruitlessly at the front of his jacket, as if he thought he was unzipping it. There was no blood, just goose down spilling out, but I choked back a sob at the sight of the bullet's entry hole.

"Please be okay," I squeaked out. My voice was clogged with tears and I fumbled at his coat with shaking fingers, searching for the zipper. "You're the doctor and none of us can help you, so you have to be okay, dammit."

There was a commotion: Darlene's scream, Maggie's expletive, followed by John's voice coming up beside me.

"John!" I cried, torn between elation and devastation. John was alive somehow, but Gabriel was shot.

Behind me I heard Darlene's hiccuping cries as she stood over the man I'd killed. I couldn't bring myself to look, especially when the baby's wails joined with hers, a chorus of choking despair. Gabriel was too important and nothing else mattered until I knew whether I'd be joining her in her grief.

"Shit, I wasn't fast enough," John said, dropping to his knees beside me, eyes wide and chest heaving. "When I realized the guy wasn't going to give up, I decided to head for my hiding space to take him by surprise once he broke the door down. But then he never came in."

"Walkie..." Gabriel gasped in a strained voice as I finally helped him pull down the zipper. I spread open the coat and ran my hands over his chest. His completely unblemished and intact chest.

"What the hell?" I rasped, tears suddenly pouring down my face, the fat droplets soaking into the material where I'd expected to find a chest wound.

He reached into his inner pocket and pulled out the now-destroyed walkie-talkie. "I told you this would come in handy," he said with a weak smirk. His eyes were bright with fear though, perhaps because he knew I was about to tackle him into the snow, raining kisses over his face.

"I thought you were dead, you asshole!" I shouted before grabbing him by the collar and pulling his face toward mine. Our kiss wasn't sexy and was probably not very pretty to watch, but the warmth that stole through my body when his lips touched mine was the stuff of legends. He wasn't dead. He was here, and he was mine.

"Where's my kiss?" John asked, scratching at the side of his nose as he kneeled beside us.

I sat up and grabbed him, pulling him into a bone-crushing hug. I barely saw him through my tears, which wouldn't stop falling. Their salty warmth stung the cut on my cheek, but John was alive and Gabriel was alive and a little pain was nothing compared to that. "You need to stop scaring the shit out of me," I whispered on a sob.

"You need to stop molesting my brother while my parents are watching," he whispered back.

I turned and saw Maggie walking alongside a tall,

sturdy woman and shorter, slim man. They had aged since their wedding photo, and both were looking worse for the wear, but they were unmistakably the elder Seongs.

John and I helped Gabriel to his feet and the family converged on one another, hugging, crying and speaking excitedly in Koringlish. Gabriel hadn't let go of my hand, but I stood outside the circle as they greeted one another.

As his father reached up to lovingly pat his face, Gabe tugged me close to him. "Appa, Umma, this is—"

"John's roommate!" I interrupted. A different kind of fear made my belly flip. I was happy to have his parents back alive and well, but everything would change now. Once again I felt like an interloper, but this time an interloper who was banging my hosts' son.

"My girlfriend," Gabriel said, and hugged me tighter.

"The girlfriend who just saved his life," John chimed in as he hugged me from the other side.

"And mine, too," Maggie added, joining the group hug.

His parents both looked at me with confusion and hesitation. Obviously, a lot had changed while they'd been gone.

"You know how to cook?" his mom asked, scrutinizing my face.

I nodded.

"You know how to clean?"

I nodded again, trying to be polite although I thought these were maybe the least important questions she could be asking, given that they'd just escaped captivity and there was a body on the ground behind us.

"What about canning? You need to know canning," she said, and that's when I snapped.

"Okay, I'm sorry. I'm really glad you're back, but I can't deal with this right now." My words flowed out in a hectic jumble as the events of the last few minutes began to overwhelm me. "I spent the morning thinking Maggie was dead, and then thinking John was dead, and then seeing Gabriel get shot, and I just killed someone. There's a woman grieving, and I think that baby needs a diaper change. Can we save the twenty questions for later?"

There was a long, loaded silence, and then Mrs. Seong stepped forward and embraced me. She squeezed me with that golden ratio of firmness to tenderness that can unexpectedly unlock a Pandora's box of emotions in the recipient. I felt a brief flash of guilt, thinking of my parents, but I imagined them in their garden hugging a lost and lonely young woman who needed them as much as I needed the Seongs. I didn't know when I would see them again, but I would.

I'm okay, and you're okay too.

"I think you'll fit in just fine," Mrs. Seong said. I don't remember bursting into tears, but I did, clutching at this woman who knew how to hug in that way specific to a certain type of mother: good ones.

We still didn't know what lay ahead. There was a body to deal with, a widow and her baby to console and a new family dynamic that would certainly have its ups and downs. But in that moment, I couldn't help but feel just a little optimistic. No matter what was happening in the wider world, we would make it.

EPILOGUE

I was being super creepy, but I didn't care. What was a little voyeurism when you had blood on your hands? Besides, I had a perfectly good reason for spying on Darlene in the middle of the night; I'd killed her husband only a week before. Since I was the last person she'd want to talk to, it was my only recourse.

I kept my step light, although I doubted she could hear me over the baby's hiccuping cries. I'd always thought of newborns as fragile things, easily breakable, but the sheer force behind his yowling amazed me every time. He was like a tourist who didn't understand a foreign language and believed that speaking louder was the only way to communicate.

I peeked through the cracked door of what used to be Maggie's room and was greeted with a heartrending sight. Darlene held the baby, still unnamed, out in front of her. She was crying as hard as he was. "I changed your diaper. I fed you. I don't know what you want from me." Her voice was brittle, and her appearance matched it. We had spoken about zombies before she arrived, and if a stranger stumbled across her now he might mistake her for one. She wasn't handling her newly widowed status well at all, and each day she grew more distant, despite the fact that the house was at full capacity.

Goddamn it.

I was tired of guilt and walking on eggshells—Dale had forced my hand when he'd attacked John and Gabriel, and I'd never forgive him for it. Taking someone's life changed everything, unless you were a sociopath. I couldn't jokingly yell, "I'm gonna kill you!" when John stole some Twinkies from the stash Mrs. Seong had given me in the hopes of cheering me up. We'd all learned the hard way that those words now resulted in a breakdown. I couldn't go a day without second-guessing myself and wondering if I should have taken some other course of action. I couldn't sleep while a fatherless child cried and an overwhelmed mother came apart like a fraying rope that couldn't be mended. I was tired, and I was actually tempted to march into the room and take the baby from her. To smooth her hair down and tell her to get some sleep. I knew there was formula in the cellar...

I'd always considered babies parasitic moochers, and now I wanted nothing more than to snatch up that scared little guy and give him affection. My, how things changed when the world stopped spinning.

I sighed and tiptoed away from the door. Maybe one day, but not tonight.

I headed down to the kitchen to make some tea that would trick my brain into sleeping. I didn't want to carry my angst into the bed I shared with Gabriel. I knew he would comfort me; he'd proven that to me every night since Dale's attack and the elder Seongs' return. The method varied—sometimes he read aloud to me from the stash of romance novels we'd found in the back of a closet. Mrs. Seong had pleaded the Fifth when we'd asked her where they came from and whether she really had a thing for leopard shifters.

Other times he fucked me senseless, literally, kissing and caressing me until there was no room for nightmares of Blue Hat or Dale or future attackers. He was always able to gauge whether I needed it fast and hard or molasses slow and tender. But the best was when we talked late into the night, unspooling vignettes from the tapestry of our pre-blackout life as we lay in bed. Sharing stories about my friends and my parents, and hearing his tales of med school madness, helped make the uncertainty of our future a little easier to bear.

There was a creak behind me as I climbed onto the kitchen counter to reach a high cabinet shelf. I didn't startle at the sound. I smiled. Gabriel knew every loose floorboard in the house; his misstep was a considerate announcement of his arrival.

"Are you stalking me?" I asked. Something tickled my ankle, and I looked down to see his hands gripping the counter on either side of my feet. I grabbed the box of tea and dropped down between his arms, my ass skimming across the front of his body.

He embraced me from behind and dropped a kiss on my head. "I'm making sure you don't break your neck trying to get the teakettle." He reached above me and pulled down the familiar metal vessel that was likely older than both of us. "It's just about perfect as far as necks go, and it would be pretty hard to replace."

My angst began to recede, pushed back by the tide of adoration in his voice. He stepped away from me, and I watched him fill the kettle and place it on the camping stove. He rummaged in the cabinet and pulled out the chipped mug that was my favorite, emblazoned with the question *What's happening hot stuff?* in fuchsia bubble letters. Like the romance novels, no one in the house seemed to know where it had come from.

"If you cared so much, you'd stop putting everything on the top shelf." I gave his earlobe a nip as I passed him, then took my usual seat at the table.

"I guess I could leave it someplace more accessible, but then what would you need me for?" he asked as he took his seat across from me. The words came out playful, but I was starting to be able to differentiate between his joking and joking-to-hide-my-feels tones, and this sounded like the latter.

I walked around the table and stood behind him, running my fingers through his hair because I knew he liked it, and because I wasn't ready to put into words what he wanted to hear. "What's wrong, Doc Seong?"

His shoulders heaved and he pulled something out from his back pocket. It looked like a brochure, but as he unfolded it on the table in front of him I realized it was a map of the United States. A simple road map, like the ones they sold in convenience stores for people who refused to relinquish control to GPS. Except...

My fingers stilled in his hair.

This map had been altered—several lines had been traced across it in varying shades of ink. I wasn't close enough to read the notes that filled the margins in the chicken scratch handwriting that pegged Gabriel as a true doctor, but I could see that the various routes all started from one point in upstate New York and stretched across the map to converge at a single pinpoint in Northern California.

My parents.

"Gabriel." I wasn't sure if I actually said his name or just mouthed the word, but he looked over his shoulder at me, his golden gaze brimming with emotion.

He cleared his throat. "I just...I don't know how long this is going to last, but if things don't get better, there are plenty of ways for us to get to California. These are just a few. I was thinking we could figure out some alternatives together."

For us. Together.

I thought all of my walls had already been scaled, but Gabriel's words demolished my very last line of defense. I stood over him and wept, unabashed. My tears dripped into his hair as I crumpled forward, unable to shoulder the weighted significance of that simple map. He was gifting me the possibility of seeing my parents, of hope for the future. He was willing to leave his family, the most important thing in his life, and travel into a dangerous and unforgiving world. He'd do that for me.

Gabriel pulled me into his lap and held me as I cried, not from fear or despair, but from the bright, beautiful fluttering in my chest that left no room for darkness.

I wasn't alone. I never had been.

"I didn't mean to upset you." He used the front of his hoodie to swipe at my face. As John would have pointed out, I was a hot mess.

"Upset me? You destroyed me." He was about to protest, but I tilted my head up and captured his mouth with mine. It wasn't possible to express what he had done for me, but I tried to imbue our kiss with my gratitude and appreciation. I pulled away, finally. "Thank you."

His brow knit in confusion. "I don't understand what's going on right now, but I think it's good, so I'll roll with it."

"It's better than good." I hopped out of his lap and pulled a chair next to him to better pore over the map.

My voice was wobbly, but I managed not to cry again. "I think this trip would best be taken once things are at least starting to get back to normal. I don't want to end up in some desperate person's freezer."

He nodded, smirking a bit and revealing that hint of a dimple in one cheek. I ran my index finger over it and then looked back at the map.

"Right now your parents and John and Maggie need us. Darlene and the baby too. But we can start planning. We can be prepared to do this, together."

The teakettle screamed, and Gabriel squeezed my hand before moving to silence it. The scent of fragrant herbs wafted from our mugs as I looked over a route marked out in hot pink. I smiled.

We were going to be okay.

Acknowledgements

Colleen, Derek and Krista, three amazing writers and friends who happily share their knowledge and their insights and don't mind me dampening their shoulders when I'm in the writerly dumps.

My parents, Clyde and Earline, who've always supported me, even when I was an insufferable teenager. Especially when I was an insufferable teenager.

Maya FL, for being the best writing bud and for reminding me that getting the words on the paper is the most important thing. This book, and all my books, might still be in my head if not for you.

Alexis and Erin, for befriending a nearly mute weirdo at a NaNoWriMo meet-up and helping her find her place in the romance writing world.

Finally, awesome editor Rhonda Helms, who whipped this novel into shape and loves my characters as much as I do. I couldn't have lucked out more in finding someone who gets my drift and goes with my flow, redirecting it as needed. You rock.